CW01376224

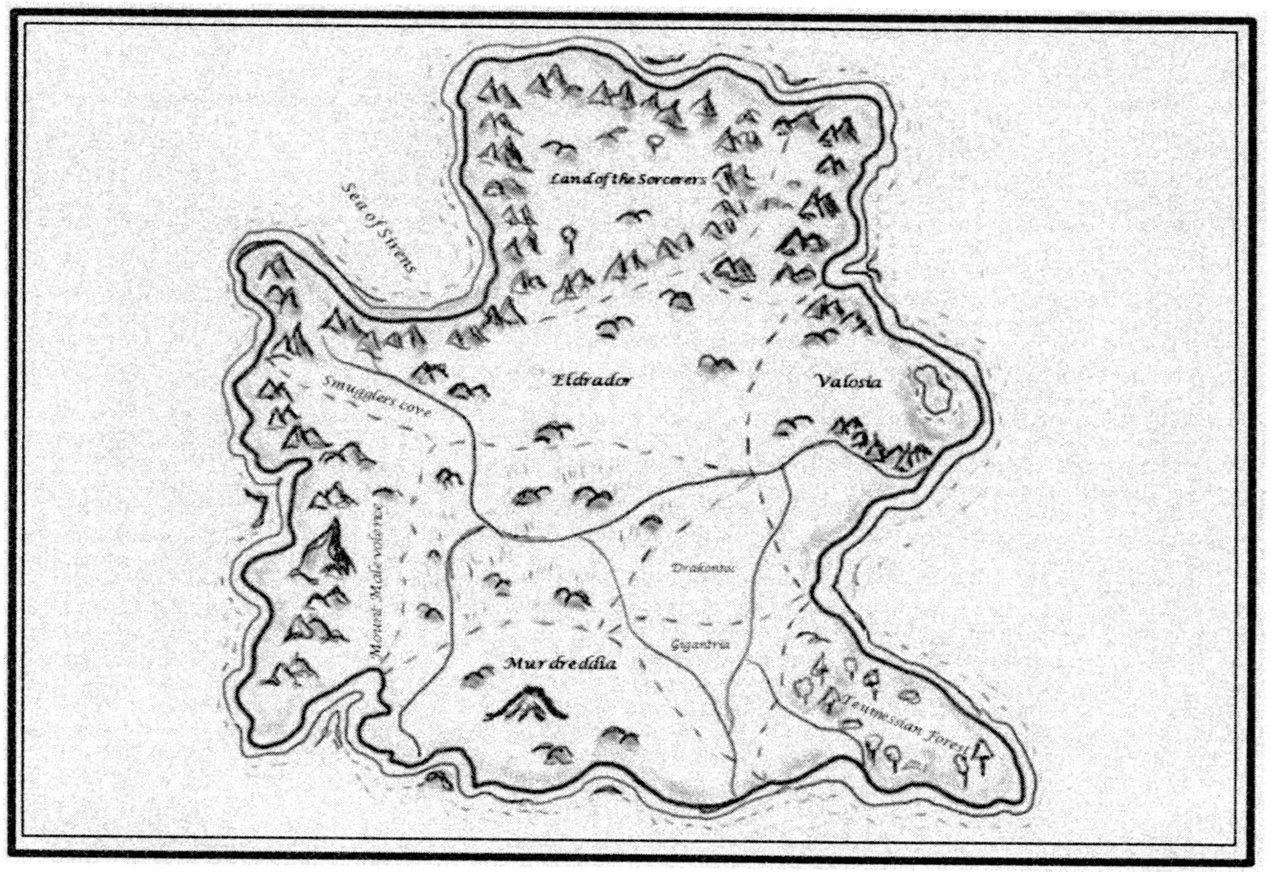
Land of the Sorcerers
Sea of Sirens
Eldrador
Valosia
Smugglers cove
Mount Malevolence
Drakonia
Gigantria
Murdreddia
Teumessian Forest

The Distant Glimmer

The Orbis Chronicles

THE DISTANT GLIMMER

Valosia

The Orbis Chronicles

Copyright © 2015 Christopher Mark Stokes

2

First Published in 2014

This second edition published in 2015

All persons depicted in this publication are entirely fictitious and any similarity to any real persons, living or dead is purely coincidental.

ISBN: 978-1-326-27487-0

Conditions of Sale

This book is sold subject to the condition that it shall not, by the way of trade or otherwise be lent, resold, hired out or otherwise circulated without the authors prior written consent in any form of binding or cover than which it is published.

The Distant Glimmer

Dedicated to my family,

The ones who believe in me.

The Orbis Chronicles

CONTENTS:

Prologue..7

The Krupto Initiative 10

An Unforeseen Delegation............................22

The Exploratory Expedition..........................32

The Distant Glimmer.....................................38

The Teumessian Forest..................................43

Murdreddia: *The Shadowed Land*....................55

Valosia 61

The Overlords Sanctuary..............................71

The Distant Glimmer

Chiron's Fate..76

Company of Ten..95

Eldrador..104

The Trolls of Mount Malevolence............116

The Land of the Sorcerer.....................129

The Soothsayer..135

Smugglers Cove..148

The Sea of Sirens.......................................162

A Returning Foe...177

The Orbis Chronicles

The Light and the Dark, the Good and the Evil...194

Friend of Foe?...215

Glossary...230

THE DISTANT GLIMMER

Prologue

*"It is a man's own mind, not his enemy or foe,
That lures him to evil ways."*

The maniacal sorcerer was dressed all in black as he moved awkwardly through the trees. His silky cape cascaded from his shoulders, waving wildly in the chill winds. Flashes of gold and dark purple surged through the air burning all that crossed their path. The dark blue leaves from the sparkling red trees burnt to cinders in an instant. The ground trembled and cracked with the forceful energy that expelled from the wooden staff, which the sorcerer clutched and wielded with his chunky, hairy fingers. He looked over his shoulder umpteen times whilst running as fast his legs could go. The sinister looking dark wizard barged through the thick, dense forestry removing everything that stood in his way, with incantations and explosive spells, which were forced from his staff. Twenty feet behind the dark wizard were three more sorcerers riding upon brilliant white destrier's, which snorted as they sprinted, forcing the warm air from their lungs to greet the cold, generating steam. The enclosing sorcerers were dressed brightly and their finely crafted cloaks glinted and glittered, under the light of the crackling pulses of energy that were still surging through the air. The destrier's hoofs kicked at dirt as they ran and the grey and silver beards of the sorcerers riding them waved in the wind lapping at their golden armoured shoulders. The dark wizard in the trees was running for his life. Everywhere was in sheer darkness and each direction looked the same. Trees were everywhere and fallen stumps and branches littered the area. Suddenly a thunderous sound was heard finding its way through the forest and for a brief while everywhere became illuminated by a bright red light. The central sorcerer riding the largest of the white destrier's had unleashed an unnaturally powerful spell. The dark wizard ceased running and he fell to the ground. He was clutching a large glass spherical object which had a multitude of colours swirling around within it. The object rolled along the uneven ground and finally rested against a rock. The sorcerer who had unleashed the spell pulled at the reins of his destrier to stop it running, its hoofs dug deep into the frosty ground. All three sorcerers stopped and climbed down from their destrier's still clutching their staffs, as if they were uncertain of what was to come. "You were warned of what would befall you, we have all been angered by your dark magic!" said the tall sorcerer as he stood over the cowering dark wizard who now clawed at the ground and tried to crawl away. The tall sorcerer moved his cloak and pushed it back over his shoulder, causing it to briefly open wide in the wind, making him look important and assertive. He proceeded to crouch down and cease hold of the magical ball of light. He wrapped it in a golden cloth and turned away from the defeated enemy, then headed back toward his destrier. As he did so he gave a gentle nod toward his companions. The two sorcerers already knew what the nod meant. They raised their long staffs in a fluid and coinciding motion, before unleashing yet another bout of spells upon the already beaten wizard who lay on the ground.

The sorcerers re-grouped and rode off upon their destrier's leaving the wizard alone in the forest, unconscious and vulnerable.

1

The Krupto Initiative

'The universe is full of magical things patiently waiting for our wits to grow sharper."

Date: June 6th 2062 A.D.

Location: Earth.

The research base towered high above nigh on all of the natural elements of the expansive surrounding areas. Thousands of square feet of glass, concrete and solar panels had all been constructed to form one of the largest scientific research facilities known to man. Access to the building was almost impossible to those who did not work within it, due to it being suspended hundreds of feet above the earth's surface. It had been engineered and perfectly imagined by expert craftsman and designed following technological revelations. For the most part, the arduous task of gaining access to the facility was largely intended, with the only form of entry being a two hundred foot vertical shaft, which was accessible only with the use of a holocard; a card given to staff members upon successfully becoming part of the most advanced research team in the world.

    The facility was in the middle of nowhere. In a location under the influence of utter natural desolation, and for miles around all that could be seen were vast plains of hillside, trees, lakes, and shrubbery which were all home to forest dwelling creatures. The facility had been named, the Krupto base, with Krupto aptly meaning the word hidden in the Greek language. The Krupto base had been created by the British government, following an initiative put in place to improve the researching capabilities of scientists. The Krupto base was one of the most technologically advanced buildings ever built. Contained within the isolated base, was a taskforce of the country's most intellectually inclined scientists and astronomers, whom had shown the most promise in the early stages of recruiting.

It was on the afternoon of June 6th 2062 that one of those intellectually advanced scientists happened upon something remarkably unwonted. In the mid-section of the research facility; also known as sector 5, there was a room that contained more technology than you would have thought possible. Thousands of screens flickered wildly like a candle next to a breezy window. Fans from computers hummed and forced warm air into the atmosphere, which then in turn got carried away into the ventilation systems by high powered air conditioners. Holographic monitors hovered above shimmering white glass coated tables as if the images they displayed had been enchanted by some ancient spell. The holograms showed a concentrated and meticulous observatory view of the stars and galaxies of the universe without the need for telescopes. In the year 2062 telescopes had become a distant memory, a hazy fragment within the minds of only the older scientists. The holographic monitors had been outsourced by the government and had come to diminish the use of telescopic equipment.

The Orbis Chronicles

The room was hot and dimly lit, with the only lights visible coming from the computers and fibre optic main frames which flickered, blue and green. Sweat beaded on the brows of the scientists as they awe inspiringly pondered over the holograms, searching for new galaxies and constellations of stars which were yet to be named; and some, which were yet to be discovered. In a corner of the room which light hadn't illuminated, an old man sat behind a computer screen with a blue glare upon his wrinkled face. His expression was unchanging and stern as he worked alone at the back of the room. The man was short and bulbous and his hair was white, and uneven, almost looking as though he had cut it himself. The man's name was Quinn Lockley. Quinn was a scientist and an astronomer and had also achieved the status of professor. Professor Quinn Lockley was one of the first scientists to work at the Krupto base, with his first day being the day the base opened in the year 2048.

Professor Lockley sat in silence all alone with the other scientists painstakingly working behind him. His social skills were not his strong point. However on that afternoon, all that changed when he was forced to share a finding with the others. The computer screen in front of him suddenly became unbearably bright. The professor struggled to see what was on the screen, as a continuous stream of light poured into his dilated pupils. It had happened unexpectedly and was like nothing he had seen before. At first he put it down to a computer glitch, however after a ponderous moment and a closer inspection of the screen; he noticed nothing had changed on the screen apart from the newly born light. The professor had been monitoring the stars surrounding the earth. He was set in his ways and preferred computers to holograms, and as he had sat staring at the screen the light had appeared almost out of nowhere. It was like an enormous star had been born before his eyes. The expression on his face changed for the first time that day, and instead of boredom, he expressed shock. "Everyone!" the professor announced, at first with his words unheard under the chatter of his colleagues. He repeated his announcement louder and the other scientists stopped immediately and turned toward him.

"What is it Quinn?" one of the sweaty scientists asked with puzzlement.

"Everyone, come and look at the screen, what do you suppose this is?" the professor replied, with his eyes unblinkingly fixated upon the hypnotic light. The others scurried across the floor like a dozen rats and they grouped around the back of professor Lockley to get a look at the screen. The white glow spread across each of the faces that looked upon it.

"Looks like a Sirius star to me Quinn!" one of them said, not seeing anything fantastical about the finding.

"I thought the same... well I actually thought it was a glitch at first, but, look at the size of it compared to the surrounding stars. It's more the size of a planet!" the professor continued almost in an inaudible whisper.

"What do you think it is then Quinn?"

"I'm unsure, but that's not the question I would be asking, a more important question would be, why haven't we seen it before?" the professor replied. He turned finally in his chair to engage in eye contact with the others.

The professor's question for the others was one they did not have an answer for. The new discovery was as close to the earth as the moon itself, yet almost fifteen years of astronomical research hadn't uncovered what appeared to be a planet sized star.

"Call him?" one of the scientists said, seeming nervous as he spoke. Professor Lockley nodded his head and stood up from his chair. He moved toward another computer and it dialled a number at the touch of a button. Four large speakers had been strategically placed around the room to provide a surround sound audibility. The number dialled and eventually rang through to another computer. Through the speakers there came a deep, yet well-spoken and clear voice, "Hello, Dr Stantham speaking" the voice announced.

"Sir, Professor Lockley here, sector 5 needs your immediate assistance!"

"What is the problem sector 5?" Dr Stantham replied,

"We have a code red discovery sir!" the professor continued. The conversation ended abruptly and professor Lockley wiped the newly formed salty residue from his forehead. A code red discovery was the name given to an anomalous finding. That afternoon was the first time a code red had ever been awarded to a discovery.

***

The night arrived dark, cold and harsh and the wilderness surrounding the facility was uninviting. The moon had vanquished the sun for another day covering everywhere with a blanket of whiteness. The stars of the universe were visible without the use of technological equipment, yet strangely, the new discovery wasn't.

Professor Lockley sat around with his colleagues nervously waiting for the doors of their room to be opened. They knew that Dr. Stantham was on his way. The screen that displayed the new discovery still shone brightly. The holographic monitors had also been partnered with the computers meaning that the discovery was now being displayed as a fully examinable 3D hologram. The room was getting hotter and the scientists felt sweat clinging to their clothes.

The Distant Glimmer

Suddenly the scientists were startled as the double doors of their research room opened with a noise that sent shivers down their spine. As the doors opened, they gradually revealed the slender physique of a six foot man. His hair was jet black and flopped around weightlessly of its own accord. The man was clothed in smart attire; a pinstripe suit adorned with white lining along the lapels of his tight fitting jacket, were the most prominent of his finely crafted garments. He stepped through the double doorway and into the stiflingly hot room which accommodated the panicked scientists. Briefly he stood, with his hands clasped tightly behind his back. His green eyes carefully, yet sternly surveyed the room. Then he spoke.

"What is the code red professor?" his voice was quiet, yet soft and clear.

"Take a look for yourself sir!" the professor said as he and the other scientists parted to allow the Dr to see the holographic monitor. The light from the monitor reflected its glare onto the Dr's face as he made a slow progression towards the table, with his hands still entwined behind his back.

"Is it a star?" the Dr asked with his eyes focused on the light.

"We believe it to be something other sir, is it not too large to be a star?" the professor replied aiming the question to anyone who felt the need to answer. But no answer came. The room was silent and the Dr continued to look into the heart of the holographic image. As Dr Stantham looked at the screen with a look of absorption upon his face, millions of thoughts each second raced through his mind, yet still he couldn't determine a plausible explanation for the mystifying light.

"How much data can you collect from within this facility?" the Dr asked, as he moved his eyes to fixate them upon professor Lockley.

"We have satellites and planetary monitoring equipment already in space; we use them to monitor the stars and other planets. They provide live feeds to our computers and holographic monitors. So we should be able to reposition some of them to collect some data" the professor replied in a tone that expressed some apprehension and insecurity.

"Retrieve what you can professor, I will be back here at 2200 hours." said Dr Stantham quietly. Professor Lockley returned a gentle nod of agreement which caused sweat to fall from his brow to the floor. Dr Stantham then made his way back out of the room; albeit more hastily than he had entered.

***

Data collected:

Object Surface temperature: 20 degrees Celsius

Object Diameter: 12,000 km

Object Circumference: 40,000 km

Protective atmosphere detected, 20% oxygen

High water content visible

Reason for excess light emittance: Unknown

Time: 22:15pm

    The automatic doors were forced into action once again, sliding side wards vanishing into the walls. Dr. Stantham re-entered the room with a look of sincerity and determination engraved onto his face. The sounds of typing and the whirring sounds of computers and the holograms as they heated up, spread throughout the room. Other than those sounds the room was in silence. The scientists looked dumbfounded, and looked to be in shock. As professor Lockley finally realised that the Dr had returned, he leapt from his chair, looking dishevelled and tired.

"Sir, please follow me" the professor said before leading the Dr. to the holographic monitor.

"Were you able to collect much data professor?" the Dr. replied as he walked toward the monitor,

"We have done the best we can, but I think what little data we have collected may surprise you somewhat," the professor and Dr. Stantham then gazed into the holographic images. Flickering with a blue-grey light within the hologram was a series of numerical data and information. The satellites belonging to the Krupto base had managed to retrieve some of the most basic information about the unidentified astronomical discovery. The Dr's eyes widened as he carefully studied the data.

"Are you sure this came from the new discovery?" the Dr asked unbelieving what he had read.

"I assure you this is the correct data" the professor replied. The Dr. gave the professor eye contact and moved in closer to whisper in a stern tone.

The Distant Glimmer

"My knowledge of planetary statistics isn't as well developed as yours professor, but even I know that most of this data is the same as the planet earth" the Dr. began with a look of puzzlement and worriment upon his face.

"You are not mistaken sir, as of yet we don't know where this 'star' has appeared from, but we have come to believe that this is a new uncatalogued planet, and by looking at these statistics, I should think we have finally found something which will give the Krupto base a purpose for having been created." The professor replied with his whispered tone instilling reality in his words. The Dr. gave a subtle nod of agreement.

"I will make the call professor!"

2

An Unforeseen Delegation

Date: June 7th 2062 .A.D.

Location: Earth, United Kingdom.

The Prime Minister of the United Kingdom in the year 2062 was the genius who devised the Krupto initiative. Known more commonly as chief commander Leatherby to the scientists of the Krupto base, Giles Leatherby was one of the most powerful men in the United Kingdom. His input in fabricating the initiative for the scientific world meant that from the day the station opened, chief commander Leatherby oversaw all aspects of research. It was on June 7th 2062, that his roles as chief commander, and likewise as Prime Minister of the United Kingdom, were truly tested.

The Distant Glimmer

    The night had well and truly arrived as commander Leatherby sat at his desk in an office many miles away from the Krupto base. His eyes were heavy with the strains of exhaustion as he glanced back and forth over important documents that had been piled high ready for his consideration. His old mahogany desk adorned with a three monitor computer and projection clock, was covered in wax sealed papers and important looking brown envelopes. A disturbance of the room's eerie silence came when the computer on the desk began to notify the commander of an incoming call. He peered up over a letter and saw the screen flickering, and highlighting the words PRIVATE LINE, KRUPTO. The unexpectedness of the call caused the commander to unintentionally create a brief pause before answering the call. Through the speakers of the computer, the tinny sound of Dr. Stantham's voice was virtually audible, though not very clear.

    "Sir, Dr. Stantham speaking from the Krupto Base, I am calling you as we have an urgent code red discovery in sector 5" the Dr spoke with a contained and professional tone in his voice.

"A code red… what could possibly necessitate such a high level priority Dr?" the commander asked sounding quite perturbed.

"We have reason to believe that we may have discovered an uncatalogued planet during our astronomical research and data collection sir!" the Dr replied.

"Very well… I need you to initiate the necessary precaution process. Catalogue the finding, and protect the information; and Dr, make sure that no one, except you and sector 5 know about this. I aim to be with you no later than 0900 hours tomorrow morning." The commander concluded. Dr Stantham acknowledged his duties and ended the call.

***

A deafeningly loud sound of a helicopters blades cutting through the cold morning air was heard above all other audible sounds. Sector 5 hadn't rested since the discovery on the day prior. Dr Stantham had also paid heed to the commander's instructions and only he and sector 5 knew of the discovery.

The sound of the helicopter startled the sector 5 scientists and their tired state made what they were hearing hurt their ears. Dr Stantham walked to a window within professor Lockleys research room and he saw the large jet black helicopter landing on the Krupto helipad. The blades slowed down on the copter and the noise ceased within seconds of the engine being shut off. Dr Stantham had ran from the window as the blades were slowing down. He made his way down the vertical shaft and headed for the ground floor in time to greet the commander. The doors of the helicopter slid open sideways just as an exhausted Dr. Stantham was running toward the helipad. Just as the commander stepped out onto the large square of concrete beneath him, Dr. Stantham stopped running and composed himself, returning to his professional and organized persona. The Dr. outstretched his sweating hand to greet the commander. The commander was tall and muscular and not atypical of a prime minister. "Good morning Dr." the commander said with his voice sounding deep and assertive.

"Good morning sir" the Dr. replied exchanging the courtesies.

"You look tired Dr. I hope this discovery isn't making you ill" the commander said with an uncomfortable smirk upon his rigid face.

"No sir, I am merely passionate about our work" the Dr. replied.

"We need to discuss this discovery Dr. but first I need to go to my office and take care of some other work, shall we convene in the board room in two hours?" the commander asked before pulling back the sleeve of his long black overcoat to check his watch.

"That sounds fine sir, it will give us more time to prepare our data" the Dr. replied in agreement.

The commander had an office within the Krupto base. It was rarely used however, as the commander's presence at the base was somewhat of a rarity. The office was at the very top of the building; it was a room on its own and was the last one to have been built when the base was constructed.

***

Time: 11:10am

The Distant Glimmer

The sector 5 board room began to gradually fill with each of the scientists that had been working on the discovery. Professor Lockley and Dr. Stantham also entered the room and awaited the arrival of the commander. The holographic monitor in the centre of the board room was loaded up and soon the 3D image of the uncatalogued object flickered and glowed among the numerical and astronomical data that had been collected by the sector 5 scientists.

The room sat in silence for over ten minutes until the commander finally arrived. He entered the room along with two other men. They were tall and dressed in finely crafted garments. Long red leather overcoats draped to the floor, and they both wore tightly fitting dark brown leather waistcoats, accustomed by boots of matching colour and dark red ties that neatly caressed their necks. They looked smart but the Dr. couldn't place them and thought it strange that he hadn't seen them leave the helicopter with the commander.

"Commander, so glad you are here, but if you don't mind my asking, who are these two gentlemen?" the Dr. asked curiously. The commander looked pale and seemed to take a little longer to answer such a simple question than he should have. But eventually he produced a smile,

"These are like my bodyguards, I take them everywhere with me, you can never me too careful when you hold such a high place in society Dr." the commanders answer made the Dr. feel more at ease though he still questioned to himself why this was the first time he had seen them.

"Do you feel alright commander, you look… a little pale?" the Dr. continued worried about the commander's sudden change in complexion.

"I'm fine Dr. I'm probably coming down with a cold or something, nothing to fret about… now, shall we proceed?" the commander replied moving the conversation onto a topic other than himself. Dr. Stantham nodded in agreement and the commander seated himself at the head of the table with a direct view of the central holographic images.

Dr. Stantham explained in depth for quite some time what the scientists of sector 5 had discovered. A lot of what was being said seemed to pass over the commanders head. His oddball bodyguards seemed to be taking more of it in than the commander himself. After a two hour long discussion in what started to become an uncomfortable and overbearingly hot room, the commander finally knew more about what had been discovered, and why it had been given a code red status.

"Well… who would have thought all those years ago when this base was created that we would find something such as this… a new planet, so close to our own both physically and scientifically." The commander began as he sat slouched in one of the leather chairs with the two stern looking men looming over him. "I will need to think on this a little, I will get back to you with where we go from here, most likely via some sort of letter or electronic mail." The commander continued before rising awkwardly from his seat. It wasn't the response the scientists and Dr. Stantham had expected, there was something about the commander that seemed queer.

"Yes sir of course" Dr. Stantham began keeping up his façade of politeness toward the commander. "Would you like me to walk with you to your helicopter?" the Dr. asked.

"NO!" the commander shouted then seemed to regret it instantly, the Dr. was also a little perturbed and shocked by the harsh response, "I mean… no,

The Orbis Chronicles

I'm fine Dr. apologies for raising my voice, I must be coming down with something. I'll be in touch soon" the commander then lowered his head seemingly ashamed of his outburst. He was then ushered out of the board room by the two red guards.

"Well… that was strange" professor Lockley said as he sat looking dumbfounded. The expressions on the faces of the other scientists weren't too dissimilar.

***

2 weeks later.

Dr. Stantham was the one to receive the response from the commander. It came in the form of an old piece of parchment sealed with red wax adorned with the emblem of the commander; a golden image of the planet earth accustomed by a golden telescope and the commanders initials 'C.L'. It had all been very well presented though the Dr. still didn't understand why the commander wouldn't revisit the Krupto base in person, following such a high level finding.

The Distant Glimmer

The Dr. sat quietly alone in his office and he carefully pealed opened the commanders letter. It was short and concise, however although it didn't say much, what had been written in the letter, was enough to turn the Doctor's complexion as white as a sheet. The letter read;

Dear, Dr. Bernard Stantham,

Following careful consideration and plentiful amounts of sincere thought, following the finding of the uncatalogued planet discovered by sector 5, within the scientific research facility known as the Krupto base, I have been able to reach only one conclusion and provide only one answer in relation to how we further this matter.

My continuing work with both you and your team has allowed me to ensure that you are more than suitable for the task I would need you to carry out. The discovery of an uncatalogued planet with scientific data so closely related to our own, planet earth is a rarity. It is this fact that has caused me to want this planet researching and exploring as closely as possible. My reasoning for this letter is this, you and a team of your choice taken from sector 5, will be required to go on an exploratory expedition to said uncatalogued planet to collect data and uncover as much information as possible, information that cannot be collected from any scientific facility. This planet may have a large impact on the future of the human race, so I say this; our future may very well lie in your hands.

Yours sincerely, Commander Leatherby,

The subject of this letter is non debateable.

The Dr. placed the letter down on the glass desk before him and ran his hands through his hair. Shock, was one of the emotions that had begun swirling around within his mind as he absorbed what he had just read. He asked himself umpteen questions in that very brief period of time, "Why would he want me and my team to go on such an expedition?" "Has the planet been researched enough?" "Is it safe?" but the one question he should have been asking himself was, why didn't the commander delegate such a mission in person?

3

An Exploratory Expedition

"Space exploration is a force of nature unto itself that no other force in society can rival."

Three weeks later:

On the hot afternoon of June 29th 2062 A.D the six members of the newly named 'Fortis' team were awaiting the beginning of their expedition into space. Dr. Stantham had informed his team of what the letter from the commander had said and he had later chosen the five men whom he wanted to accompany him on his expedition. Five men who worked within sector 5 of the Krupto base. Following the letter Dr. Stantham had heard no more from the commander. Two days after the letter had been read there was a high security delivery sent to the Krupto base. It was one of the world's most technically advanced space crafts. The space craft was jet black, the same as the commander's helicopter had been. The craft had been expertly crafted and configured in the shape of the letter 'T' with an elongated cargo bay fluidly flowing into two right and left hand side sections with drive units and escape pods. Tinted black windows and a matt anti-gleam coating completed the aesthetically pleasing construction along with the golden earth emblem of the commander and a large silver letter 'K' which stood for Krupto. The space craft had been prepared outside near the Krupto base helipad. It was a sight to behold and was somewhat prepossessing, the size of the space craft was also awe-inspiring. Dr. Stantham had grouped with his team not too far away from the craft. The majority of scientists working at the Krupto base also now had their suspicions about what was taking place, and conjectures and questions were rife on the day that the expedition was due to begin. Dr. Stantham and his team all looked smart and prepared for what lay ahead; even if they didn't quite feel prepared. The Fortis team had been outfitted in state of the art space suits, which had been made to protect the team against the strains of space and the uncertain toxicity of the atmosphere on the planet they were being forced to explore. The suits were also black with red linings and pockets aplenty, they had also been given aerodynamic helmets with 360 degree viewing angles, which eliminated any blind spots for the wearers. As the team stood looking up at the spacecraft Dr. Stantham felt it was his duty to speak to his team before the expedition began,

"I know you must be experiencing some nervousness and possible nausea at this point gentlemen. I can assure you, I am too. I just wanted to thank you all for agreeing to do this with me, I still am unsure about why it was that I was asked to carry out such an expedition, but I had no choice but to follow the orders I was given, and doing this may be result in our future becoming reformed" said the Dr, as he gave his fellow crew members all the encouragement he could give. The Dr. gave a proud glance toward his team. On the far left of the Dr. there was a familiar face, Professor Lockley; the man who had discovered the uncatalogued planet. Naturally, he looked nervous, but nevertheless seemed to be eager to find out what the place he had discovered was going to be like. Standing next to the Professor was a younger man with black spectacles and short blonde hair, his name was Professor John Cumbridge; although he was young he was very bright and knew much about the universe. Directly in front of the Dr. was Dr. Stantham's very own son. It was his only child, but he had recently become involved in the same work as his father, he was not yet a Professor or a Dr however he was very well educated, and his father had taught him well. Dr. Stantham had first objected to him being part of the team, and he would have preferred him not to be going on the expedition, but his son was insistent and a man old enough to make his own decisions. He was twenty five years of age, handsome and had a thick black Quiff of hair. His name was Étoile Stantham; his name meant Star in French so he had been aptly named by his father. Two more men remained, they were stood to the right of the Dr. They were brothers, and they had a long history of working together to find the most curious discoveries in the universe. Their names were Michael and Gordon Carlson. They were both quite short and were rather portly, they were also nigh on identical, but their appearances didn't stop them having unmatched intellectuality and a high grade scientific ability.

They were six of the best scientists that the Krupto base had to offer, however they had never before journeyed beyond the boundaries of the earth's atmosphere.

8:52pm June 29th 2062,

The space craft was eventually fired up and an overbearing smell of fuel poured into the air from its rear Ion Drive. The night was also beginning to creep in and the moon cast its light upon the untouched cleanliness of the spacecraft's exterior. Soon one of the scientists working on the craft came forth to tell Dr. Stantham that it was time for them to board.

"Thank you, follow me gentlemen… it's time!" said the Dr.

No one else spoke as they followed the worker to the deployed ramp which led them up into the spacecraft. Soon they boarded the craft one by one, the last person to board the space craft was Dr Stantham, and he gave one final glance toward the Krupto base then turned to enter the craft.

The ramp rose to seal the spacecraft, so tight that oxygen itself could not escape. Inside the spacecraft there were a row of six seats, a control panel and an area to use the toilet, alongside this there were many rooms hidden behind sliding doorways. The interior of the craft was pristine and glimmered with a blinding whiteness. Holographic computer systems and touchscreen walls and table tops were also plentiful. There was also a large wide window at the front of the space craft which would allow the team to look out at the stars that they would soon be surrounded by. Finally the team strapped themselves in with shaking hands and prepared themselves for what was to come.

9:00pm June 29th 2062,

As each member of team Fortis sat in their seats staring out of the large tinted window there came an automated voice from the spacecraft's interior speaker system. The voice began announcing the final moments before the expedition.

"*One minute until launch sequence,*" was the voices first announcement, but eventually the voice began to announce the final countdown " *seconds until launch sequence,*"
10…9…8…7…6…5…4…3…2…1, *launch sequence engaged!*" As each crew member sat gripping the arms of their seats the crafts rear Ion Drive began to force into action sending fierce blasts of fuel into the cold night air. The amount of force being given off began to lift the craft from where it was

standing. In a matter of seconds the craft had left the Krupto base behind, causing it to gradually decrease in size. The spacecraft neared the earth's atmosphere.   Inside the crew members looked out at the clouds that grew nearer to them until eventually they pierced them, and made a harsh exit from the planet earth, forcing their way through the ice cold atmosphere and into the universe of stars, galaxies, black holes, planets and a vast open endless entity of space. The spacecraft was finally free to proceed on its course toward the new planet.

Miles away from home the journey began…

4

The Distant Glimmer

The beginning of the journey started with a long drawn out silence. No one spoke, and all that could be heard was the odd beeping noise from the control panel ahead of them. It seemed as though everyone had become hypnotised by what they saw. Outside the spacecraft all that could be seen was darkness sprinkled with bright stars and purple mists of various galaxies which treated the eyes with their beauty. They couldn't quite believe just how close to the stars they were; the stars that they had very often monitored with the latest technological equipment. All that could be tasted was the air that they breathed from within their helmets, and a feint smell of fuel lingered in the cabin for quite some time.

The first to speak was Dr Stantham with his voice sounding muffled beneath the glass of his helmet, "it should be approximately 48 hours until we reach the destination that has been programmed into the spacecraft" he said reassuringly. Each one of the crew members seemed to express regret on their faces, a fear of the unexpected gripped them all. The Dr's son Étoile unbuckled his belt and went to explore the spacecraft in its entirety. State of the art artificial gravity within the spacecraft meant that he was able to walk around freely as though he were still on earth. The others continued to stay seated near the main control panel. They studied everything they saw. Each member of the team had been trained and prepared for an exploratory expedition; it was required under the new laws, however, not one of them had ever thought that they would be the ones required to physically undertake such a mission.

    Michael and Gordon had soon slunk into their seats and had dozed off trying to pass some time away; Professor Lockley glanced back and forth over the control panel with an attentive eye. The beginning of the journey started with slow progression and soon tedium possessed each member of the crew.

***

…Meanwhile not too far away, unbeknownst to the Fortis crew, there was another spacecraft following them closely behind. The spacecraft contained some familiar looking men. They were the finely dressed, supposed bodyguards, of the commander. Two of the men on board the craft were the ones who had been standing behind the commander during the sector 5 briefing.

The two men from the briefing were still dressed in their red and brown leather attire and they seemed to be the ones in charge of the craft. They sat in large silver V shaped chairs monitoring highly advanced holographic systems and large touch screen controls. The men hadn't been introduced to the Fortis team during the briefing of sector 5 because there purpose for being there was most likely not because of them being bodyguards. The men looked like soldiers, strong and stern with one apparent objective; staying hot on the tails of the Krupto spacecraft. The soldiers in red now also sported golden name tags which were pinned to the lapels of their red leather overcoats. They seemed to be using them like a soldier's dog tag, to be identifiable, almost as if they were all strangers to one other. The two men from the sector 5 briefing had strange names; names not usually heard in relation to people in any country on earth. One of them was called Akaz, he looked pale and his hair was long and wet looking, he also wore three golden stars on his opposite lapel, signifying some sort of top ranking among the strange men. The other man from the sector 5 briefing was Brimir, he looked as stern as his colleague, but one if his eyes was permanently sewed shut, most likely an old war wound. Brimir had a two star silver badge on his lapel which showed his second in command ranking among the men. The remaining men all wore bronze singular star badges on their lapels, and they had names such as, Gallar, Helgrind, Kolga and Runa. The crew of red soldiers also consisted of six men, which perfectly balanced out against the Fortis crew. The space craft of the red soldiers was almost twice as large as the Krupto craft, and its interior seemed more technically advanced with technology which would not be found in even the most advanced facilities on earth. The space craft was filled with hundreds of cabinets made from tempered glass, which had been loaded with weaponry; enough to start a dozen wars. The reasons for such vast amounts of weaponry, and for following the Fortis crew were as of yet, entirely unknown.

***

The Orbis Chronicles

46 Hours Later:

Aboard the Krupto spacecraft, Dr. Stantham was the only one still awake. The others had all drifted off into a slumber most likely due to the lack of activeness and the inability to occupy their minds. Dr Stantham however had not gone to sleep but had instead sat with a look of nervousness and terror upon his face. Occasionally he looked at the many buttons that flickered and flashed on the control panel, he also gazed out into the stars and wondered if what he and his team were doing, was the wisest decision. He also sat with his mind plagued by thoughts of the commander's sudden decision to devise such an expedition at such short notice. However, it was during his brief period of questionable thought, he returned to look out of the window, when something finally caught his eye that wasn't a star or a galaxy like he had been looking at since the beginning of the journey. Immediately he awoke the team to show them what he had begun to see in the distance. To ensure his eyes were not tricking him he asked Professor Lockley if he could also see the distant object, with a reply of "yes" from the Professor, they realised that what they were looking upon, was the mysterious planet which they had come on the

The Distant Glimmer

expedition to find. A faint white glow pulsated amidst the surrounding stars, a light which grew ever bigger as they drew nearer.

5

The Teumessian Forest

The painfully bright light continued to draw ever nearer to the Krupto space craft. The Fortis crew members could now feel sweat collecting on their foreheads and the rate at which their hearts were beating had almost doubled in a matter of moments. Dr. Stantham rose up from his chair at the front of the craft and moved to a touchscreen monitor on one of the walls of the craft. He pushed numerous buttons, then began using voice commands to converse with the computer. "Computer, I need you to check the suits of every person aboard this craft, check for any faults and anomalies, and make sure that they are safe to be worn outside of this craft" Dr. Stantham said as he spoke clearly into the computers microphone. The computer acknowledged the request made by the Dr. and suddenly there appeared a large rectangular holographic light. It moved up and down the entirety of the cargo bay. The blue holographic light caressed every square inch of the space craft and clung to every stitch of the crew member's space suits. Then the light dissipated in an instant. The computer then began to speak to the Dr. in an automated voice, "Analysis shows, no faults or anomalies with any of the six suits contained aboard this craft, all suits are ready for outside exploration." Dr. Stantham then turned and made his way hastily toward his chair. "O.K, I just wanted to make sure these suits are safe, that planet is nearly upon us, make sure you are strapped in, the craft should safely guide us through the atmosphere and find us somewhere to land on the planets terrain." Said the Dr. whilst reaching for his own seat belt and securing himself ready for the atmospheric impact.

The planet was soon upon them, but still they could not determine where the source of the light was coming from. The space craft automatically lowered its visors blocking out some of the light rays which had become too bright to look upon with the naked eye. The space craft entered into the planets atmospheric gravity current, and upon impact it felt as though they had crashed into an invisible wall. The craft was now beyond the point of no return and the planet's surface wasn't too far away. The craft was being pulled down toward the ground. The scientists gripped their seats and closed their eyes as an unnatural force pushed their heads back into the leather of their seats. Dr. Stantham peered out of the window and saw a myriad of colours which appeared to be forming the tops of trees. They prepared for impact as the planets terrain and shrubbery drew ever nearer. The space craft's auto pilot corrected its unsteadiness and slowed down in order to carefully and precisely land upon some solid ground. The craft crashed through the brightly coloured trees and became surrounded by glittering tree stumps and red leaves. Then it landed. The ground was hard yet uneven, but, no one had been injured and the craft had successfully landed upon the surface of the new planet. All was silent. The scientists leant forward just as the crafts visors lifted once again. Light streamed through the window; a light which seemed to look like the natural sunlight back on earth. No one spoke, and their faces found it hard to settle upon one expression. No words could be conjured for what they were feeling. The one element that they couldn't quite create reasoning for was where had the bright light gone? Upon entering the planet the bright light had disappeared and it was now no more than what was perceived to be natural daylight.

THE DISTANT GLIMMER

***

Concurrently with the Krupto craft successfully landing on the surface of the planet, the space craft containing the red soldiers was also finding a place to land. On the opposite side of the forest where the Krupto craft had landed the red soldiers had begun manoeuvring their large space craft into a clearing amidst the trees. The Fortis crew had no inclination that they were being followed and the red soldiers had landed far enough away that they were still able to stay hidden from their sights. Akaz and his team exited the craft clutching onto a plethora of oddly shaped weapons that they had taken from the glass cabinets. They marched sternly through the clearing and made progression toward the covering of the forestry. The red soldiers were wearing no protective clothing as they walked across the surface of the planet, which seemed odd compared to the precautions that the Fortis team had taken to ensure they would be safe. Gravity on the planet seemed comparable to that of the planet earth as the men walked normally across the terrain, which was the first suggestion that the research that had been carried out by sector 5 had been reliable. The red soldiers reached the cover of the forest and were engulfed by the naturally formed darkness of the canopies above.

***

Dr. Stantham and professor Lockley used the internal computer systems to retrieve some last minute data and planetary statistics before they set foot outside the craft. No anomalies were found and the computer showed no reason for the doors of the craft not to be opened. The crew members each powered up their computerised helmets which produced holographic images on the inside glass, displaying mobile statistics and the status's of their suits and their bodies, such as oxygen intake and heartrate. The ramp of the spacecraft began to lower itself following a brief judder. A gentle breeze made its way into the cargo bay from the outside world and the gentle sound of rustling trees caressed the ears of the scientists. The computerised helmets continued to display statistics to ensure that they were safe to proceed. All seemed normal and no anomalies were detectable. Dr. Stantham was the first to leave the craft. His boots touched down on the ramp and he made his way toward the uneven rocky terrain that was the forest floor. The trees looked strange and were brightly coloured, they also glittered under the light of the planet. Dr. Stantham surveyed the area noticing every detail. His helmet provided him with an even closer detailed inspection of the surrounding areas; such as nearby substances and chemicals that were detectable. The remaining scientists all followed closely behind Dr. Stantham and soon grouped with him at the foot of the spacecraft's ramp. They felt the gravitational pull of the planet was not too dissimilar from earth, and the helmets were displaying the current surface temperature as being 12 degrees Celsius and 53.6 Fahrenheit; which for June was slightly cooler than expected yet wasn't too extreme. However as the scientists looked up at the skies they noticed a considerable difference. In the place of clear blue skies there instead loomed glittering balls of white light surrounded by red mists and purple swirls suspended in a canvas of soft orange light. Beyond the orange sky they could still see the stars of the universe as they flickered with a blinding whiteness. It all looked quite magical and was unexpected. The ground beneath the scientist's feet was reminiscent of rigid rocks. The rocks flowed into one other, and they looked like slabs of naturally formed marble which glittered beneath the unexplainable light source. A low fog also moved along the ground and parted as the scientists began making a slow progression through the forestry, leaving the craft to stand alone amidst the trees. In the distance there were tall mountains capped with ice and streams of water could be heard nearby. The entirety of the surrounding area seemed to be coated in glitter as everything glistened with an aesthetic beauty.

    The first to speak was Etoile, his voice began to emerge from his helmet almost as a whisper, "what a beautiful place this is" he said; the Dr. looked to his son with a glint of happiness in his eyes.

    "I agree, this place truly is something that one would usually only dream about." Everyone seemed to be stunned with amazement and didn't seem to want to move. However, brothers Michael and Gordon both knew that there was more to see. They wanted to see as much as possible, and they knew standing dormant in one place could only allow them to see so much. Taking their next few steps out across the rocky terrain they began to feel at peace as sounds were seldom heard around them. As the brothers walked across the rocks they took everything in that they saw, heard and smelt around them. They held red leather journals which they had taken from their satchels. They noted down every detail as they wanted to be able to take the information back home to the commander. Each of the scientists continued to walk with slow progression. They noticed bushes and brambles imbedded into the rock but nothing seemed to be growing in dirt. Everything seemed to be able to live without the nutrients of the ground or natural sunlight. Everything they saw and came into contact with looked as if it shouldn't be able to exist, but no matter what they saw, Michael and Gordon made notes. The scientists soon noticed a gentle stream of crystal blue water gently flowing not too far away from where they were stood, they had previously heard the sounds of cascading rivulets and now they saw the cause of the sounds. The stream seemed to go on for miles ahead of them and it weaved in and then back out again as if it were going around the many trees within the forest.

However, as of yet, they hadn't seen any forms of life. The group of intrigued scientists had come to feel as if they were the only ones on the planet. Soon though, they realised that those thoughts had entered their minds a little too hastily.

THE ORBIS CHRONICLES

In the heart of the forest they began to hear a noise close by. Each of the scientists looked around in angst looking for the cause of the sudden noises. The scientists began to form a tight circle to cover all angles. There warm breath began to caress the glass of their helmets and the rhythm of their breathing increased along with their heart rates. As they stood with their nerves on edge, from behind a rock there suddenly bounded a large creature. The creature looked like a large fox, but it had a sincere look of anger dwelling in its eyes. Its bright red tail bushed up behind itself with streaks of glistening silver hair entwined into its deep red fieriness. A look of terror had formed upon the face of Dr Stantham and the others. Professor Lockley looked at the creature and the creature stared back as if it were looking into his soul. Its jaws opened to show its fangs, and drool dripped down the sides of its face. The creature moved forwards slowly with its large paws stepping unevenly across the rocks. The Professor stepped backwards to increase the distance between them. The jaws of the creature began to open wider and it seemed to begin getting into a position to attack. The hearts of the group thudded loudly and beads of perspiration greeted their brow; however, another sound was suddenly heard, and it began drawing near. Unexpectedly a large creature with the body of a horse and the torso and head of a man appeared from the darkness of some nearby trees. It scared away the large fox now leaving the group alone with the half man half horse. The large half breed creature moved cautiously toward the scientists with an incredulous look upon his hairy face. The creature was muscular and looked strong and heroic as he neared the scientists. Then to their surprise, it began to speak.

"I am Chiron, the one who patrols these forests to ensure creatures like the one you just happened upon do not come into this territory" said the creature as he began addressing the scientists in deep and authoritative tone. The fact that the creature had spoken came as a sudden shock to the scientists, however Dr Stantham took it upon himself to step forth and address the strange creature.

"Hello sir, my name is Dr. Stantham, I am the leader of this here crew, we are indebted to you for saving our lives, and if you don't mind my asking, what was that creature?" Chiron glanced down towards the Dr as he stood at least four feet higher than any of the scientists,

"That creature was a Teumessian fox; cunning creatures and equally as dangerous, but they are impossible to catch which leaves us with the constant problem of them infecting our territory with their devious behaviour". The looks of shock and confusion continued to spread their way across the faces of the company, Chiron broke the silence by aiming a question towards Dr Stantham,

"May I ask you sir, who might you be and why are you in this forest?"

The Dr. then stepped forth,

"We are strangers here, we have journey here on an expedition from the planet earth, we are scientists and we discovered this planet and found many of its statistics were the same as ours, so we came on a journey here to see it for ourselves." Chiron then looked over each of the members of the company carefully, with his big brown eyes,

"Well it seems you have come here unprepared for what you have already seen, this planet will inhabit many creatures which will not be familiar to you, and the shock you already express shows me you have not seen anything like me or that fox before!"

The Distant Glimmer

Professor Lockley stepped forward to stand beside Dr. Stantham, he swallowed the lump which had formed in his throat, then began to speak,

"We have come a long way and we are here to find out as much as possible about this planet, so that we can tell others about it back home, and what we have already seen shows us that there is now more than enough reasons for us to stay and find out more about this planet, and discover things that no one from our planet ever has. Creatures such as that fox and yourself have only been read about in mythological stories and legends back home, so I ask you Sir, will you please allow us to see more of your planet and its beauty?"

Chiron thought hard about what he was being asked and he seemed to be asking himself questions in his mind. Although he knew that they were not here to put his planet in jeopardy, he wanted to find out more about them.

"You have kind and true hearts, and you are more than welcome to see this world, but it will be dark soon as the light of the planet will be dimmed. I insist that you follow me to my home, where you will eat and rest before you see any more of this planet," Dr Stantham acknowledged Chiron and replied instantly with gratitude,

"Thank you Chiron, we appreciate your kindness sir." Chiron then gave a gentle nod and turned around to lead them to his home. They made their away across a rocky path, and through many trees and a myriad of colourful shrubbery, where they were being lead was uncertain, they were also unsure about whether or not they could trust the large creature, but they felt confused and nothing had prepared them for what they had happened upon.

***

The red soldiers continued to traverse the terrain of the planet, with their weaponry and there stern and emotionless expressions. The direction they were heading in was different to the direction that Chiron was leading the scientists, however, their destination was clear to them, and the speed at which they made progression and their assured focus on their objective showed that they had some familiarity with their surroundings.

6

Murdreddia – The Shadowed Land of Old

"We are nearing my home gentlemen" said Chiron as they awkwardly made their way across the hard terrain. Soon they neared another area of forestry. The trees they now looked upon however looked different to the ones in the Teumessian forest. Each tree looked precious and looked to have been standing for many a century. Each one had silver branches with glistening red leaves clinging onto them. Every direction surrounding the scientists, was inhabited by more trees of varying variety. The scientists also noticed nearby, the end of the stream which they had first noticed in the Teumessian forest. They walked with their eyes unable to look upon everything. There was so much to see that they had never been witness to before, and every minutiae detail of the planet seemed blessed with natural grace and elegance.

The Orbis Chronicles

The company of scientists soon were brought to a halt in front of a large stone archway which stood tall surrounded by the many trees. The archway had been perfectly carved out of white stone and had become entwined in dark green vines. Chiron turned and looked at the scientists making them feel more at ease with a gentle a smile, "this archway is the gateway to my realm. Upon entering this archway you will find yourself within a town, bustling with centaurs like myself. Don't be afraid, they will be your friends as long as you are with me, and as long as you treat them respect!"

Dr Stantham then peered up at the tall centaur,

"Of course, we will respect anyone and anything beyond this archway, we appreciate what you are doing for us."

Chiron smiled in the direction of the company of scientists before once again turning towards the stone archway and walking through it, leaving the scientists by themselves once again. Before following Chiron, Étoile looked up and noticed an inscription imbedded within the stone of the archway, it read *'Valosia Valtakunta Rauhan Jakoti Tarnhelm'*
Although they did not know what this meant they did not query it. They proceeded cautiously through the archway and into the hidden realm. Dr.

The Distant Glimmer

Stantham led the way as they shuffled through the archway to find out what awaited them beyond.

***

The red soldiers cut through trees and snapped fallen branches with their heavy boots as they continued on their chosen pathway. They were still clutching the weapons which they had previously taken from their craft and their heads were now being concealed by large hoods. Soon they strayed from the forest floor and found themselves on a dark rocky path which had become surrounded by black brambles and dark purple trees that didn't glisten under the light, but instead were covered in red thorns and green mouldy decay. Akaz walked the length of the pathway followed closely by his armed crew members. As they walked the light of the planet seemed to become dimmer and dimmer with each passing second, and then suddenly it diminished entirely. In seconds what was thought to be daylight had vanished and it had now been replaced by dark skies and purple mists. The stars of the universe out yonder were also brighter and more prominent than before. The day was gone and in its wake, was a black canvas of darkness.

The red soldiers were undeterred by the dramatic transition between day and night. They looked unfazed and quite at home.

A faint light soon became visible ahead of the red soldiers. The light was highlighting some kind of entrance. Akaz turned to his men and addressed them with sincerity "We have arrived, the Overlord awaits us!"

The voice of Akaz was spine chilling. His fellow soldiers gave thin smiles as he spoke showing that they were pleased about something.

The entrance that Akaz had led his team to, had been lit by large red candles that dripped hot wax down the length of dirt and mould ridden crumbling walls. The entrance was in the form of a wooden door. The door had old rusty hinges and was adorned with the words *'Varjostama Maa Vanha'* The words meant 'The Shadowed Land of Old,' and Akaz read them as he stood at the door, as though he knew what they meant. Akaz stepped forth and knocked thrice on the door, and a small rectangular cut out in the wood then slid sideways, and an old man with green eyes and long wet grey hair clinging to his scalp peered through at the red soldiers. No words were exchanged between the two and the old man, who was seemingly a guard at the entrance, once again closed the peep hole. The door's hinges creaked and dust flew out and escaped into the darkness as the entrance began opening inward. Cobwebs were also broken as the door opened, showing the door hadn't been used for some time. Akaz led his men through the entrance and passed the old man. The old man stared at them with a hint of recognition as they passed, but no words were exchanged. The entrance guard then turned to the door before bolting it shut. Akaz walked with his men following him closely with their large weaponry in their hands. The realm they had entered into, was not easy on the eye, and no aesthetic beauty had awaited them beyond the door. Every square inch of the realm was shrouded in preternatural darkness. The ground had turned to dirt and the glistening marble rocks had disappeared. The ground was flat as if a hundred heavily armoured men had trampled over it with their boots. The air smelled damp and felt heavy, and all that could be heard were the sounds of what seemed like the cawing of crows or creatures of a similar sound. Mounds of rock stood high and smoke bellowed from them like chimney pots, and instead of pools of crystal clear cool water, there were instead boiling red and orange lava pits which glowed amidst the dark territory. There were also various strategically placed candle holders that flickered with candles burning bright. The pits of lava that were glowing as far as the eye could wander, were each adjoining to a volcanic mountain of enormity that was seen in the distance. Volcanic ash also filled the air, and added to the eeriness of the dark realm which Akaz had brought his men.

As the red soldiers continued to walk, out of the shadows there suddenly appeared a large black creature. It looked like a horse, but it had large black wings resting at its sides and its eyes were filled with what looked like red and orange flames. It breathed heavily and dark smoke bellowed from its nostrils. The creature was a ghost horse, loyal servants of the overlord, a creature without a soul. In its place lurked an unprecedented evil. As the horse stood it occasionally flickered like a candle near a breeze, exposing its skeletal structure, as if it was stuck in a rift between life and death. However, Akaz and the others had no fear of the ghost horse; the fear that resided within them had been awakened by the sight they saw atop the horse. It was the rider of the ghost horse that they had focused their attention on. The rider was a tall man with skin as white as pearls. He was clad all in black from head to toe, with a large hood and a flowing long cape that sat over the back end of the horse. His eyes were empty and had no colour. They were jet black except for the whites of the eyes.

A deep voice suddenly came from the dark creature, "Akaz!" its voice boomed and echoed through the air "It's been a while, Malvo wishes to see you!" Akaz nodded in the direction of the dark man and gave no response. The red soldiers then watched as the ghost horse spread its wings and flew off into the direction of the large volcano with the dark being upon its back. Akaz turned to the other men with fear dwelling within his eyes,

"We should hurry, Malvo is expecting us!" they then made their way across the dirt covered paths, and headed in the direction of the volcano, with the weight of the air and the volcanic ash pressing down on them.

The Orbis Chronicles

T

Valosia

ValosiaValtakunta Rauhan JakotiTarnhelm
(Valosia, the realm of peace and the home of the Tarnhelm)

Dr Stantham was the first to pass through the stone archway closely followed by Professor Lockley. The others came through immediately after one another, until eventually the entire company of scientists was standing within the realm of Valosia. They stood side by side with their backs facing the stone archway. They stared out at the sites that they now saw before them, with the sound of running water nearby. The birthplace of the stream was a Cliffside waterfall that stood high above the village below. Rivulets of cool refreshing water flowed from the waterfall and cascaded below into calm lakes and gentle streams. The realm of Valosia was of an immeasurable size, and was under the influence of utter natural serenity. The uneven rocky terrain of the planet, had turned to a smooth flat surface, which gleamed still even though the planet had now turned to darkness. For the first time since they had arrived on the planet, the scientists now saw homes standing side by side hand carved from white stone. Smoke poured out of chimney tops and fires from within the homes glowed against the windows with an orange warmth. Red bushes with golden petals were situated in many places around the homes and everything that was looked upon caused those who looked upon it to become overwhelmed with a feeling of peace and tranquillity. The beauty which Valosia beheld was something unimaginable.

    As the scientists stood near the archway with looks of amazement upon their faces, they were taken from there trance when they were greeted by a female centaur. Long brown hair flowed down the back of the beautiful creature, and her bright blue eyes captured the light of the candles which stood nearby. The hair upon her body looked as if it were made from brown silk. She glanced her eyes toward Dr Stantham and spoke with a soft voice, "hello gentlemen, my name is Alaya, I am the daughter of Chiron. My father wishes for you to convene with him at our home, so that you can eat and drink, and so that you can tell us more about yourselves." Dr Stantham stepped forth and reached out his hand to shake Alaya's and to greet her in the kindest of ways.

"Thank you Alaya, we will be more than happy to adhere to your father's request, you have all been more than generous since our arrival on this planet," replied the Dr. Alaya produced a smile, then led them across a smooth marble path toward the home of Chiron.

Eventually the home of Chiron was in sight, it was like no other home they had ever seen. It stood before the cascading waterfall and towered over the entirety of the adjacent village. It looked like a castle. Part of the exterior of the home consisted of turrets and hundreds of windows of all shapes and sizes. It had also been carved out of the same white stone as the other homes, but its size, and the expert craftsmanship that had produced it, told the scientists that Chiron held a place of high importance within the realm. The stone walls of the large house had centaurs from times of old, carved into them, and above the main door were again the words from the archway, '*Valosia Valtakunta Rauhan Jakoti Tarnhelm.*' The company of scientists stood at the foot of the stone steps which led up to the main door with expressions of awe upon their faces.

"Come gentlemen, my father awaits you," said Alaya before making her progression toward the main entrance. The first of the scientists to follow Alaya were Michael and Gordon. They were the most excitable of the company and also the most curious. They were closely followed by the remaining scientists. The steps which they climbed seemed never ending and each stride seemed to work every muscle in the legs. Eventually they reached the peak of the stone steps and soon were stood face to face with an enormous golden doorway surrounded by white candles. The face of Chiron was suspended in a golden Muriel aloft of the doorway. Dr Stantham stepped forth and pushed the door inward revealing the large marble hallway which lay within. The Dr stepped through the door and instantly noticed a myriad of many portraits and paintings adorning the walls either side of the hallway. At the far end of the hall loomed a staircase which wound its way up to a second level of the enormous home. Three tables stood in the centre of the hall one after another with brightly coloured plants within golden pots standing proud on top of them. There were also more golden doorways; although not as big as the main entrance, standing in various places along the sides of the hallway. As the scientists stood taking in the enormity of the home and loosing themselves in gazes at the chandeliers above their heads, a familiar face stepped out from behind a door near the far end of the hall, it was Chiron.

"Hello Dr, I am glad to see my daughter passed on the message, come, I have had meals prepared for you and there is much I wish to ask you, there is plenty of time for you to look around my house, but I am sure you are tired and hungry" said Chiron in a soft tone. Michael and Gordon acknowledged his words and were the first to head toward the door. The Dr turned to his son Étoile and the remaining professors and gave a small grin before he himself made his way toward Chiron.

As the company passed through the small golden door they entered into another large room. A long table filled the centre of the room adorned with silver wear and dishes containing a plethora of varied food. Golden goblets also stood brimming with red wine and various ales, and large cushioned chairs surrounded the table, with enough of them to accompany at least thirty people. On the far wall their also flickered a large coal fire which crackled and spat out sparks which flew forth onto the white polished tiles of the floor. More antique paintings hung from nails on every wall of the room and another large and low crystal chandelier hung over the candelabra centre piece of the table.

Already seated at the head of the table; although not on a chair, was Chiron, accompanied by his alluring daughter Alaya. No one else occupied any of the other chairs, as it seemed that only Chiron and his daughter occupied the enormous home.

"Come in gentlemen, take a seat and feel free to feast on many of the delightful treats we have prepared for you, and feel free to remove those helmets, I feel the air will be perfectly breathable for you here!" said Chiron,

"Thank you" replied Dr Stantham, before slowly removing his helmet with a little reluctance. However, to the surprise of the Dr., Chiron was right. The air was breathable and smelled clean and fresh as he inhaled deep lungful's. The others also removed theirs in succession before seating themselves near Chiron and his daughter. Michael and Gordon reached out to a pile of what was perceived to be large chicken legs. They also reached out and picked up some potatoes before filling the plate in front of them with one of everything on the table. Michael and Gordon seemed to be lacking any form of etiquette as they sat eating their fill. Everyone sat around the table and ate and also drank a selection of varied beverages, until all that was left on the table were some vegetables, and crumbs of bread.

As the meal concluded, the first to speak again, was Chiron, "I hope you don't mind my asking Dr., but what is the real purpose for you being on this planet?" the question seemed to startle the Dr. somewhat and tiredness caused by the hearty meal had begun to shroud his mind. However, he eventually conjured a response.

"Well, as you may already know, we are an advanced team of scientists and researchers from the planet earth, we work within a secretive scientific research facility known as the Krupto base. My friend here, Professor Lockley, was the man who discovered your planet!" Chiron continued to look upon the Dr with curiosity before continuing his questioning,

"So you discovered the planet and then just decided to make your way across the universe unaware of what truly awaited you?" Chiron replied quite abrupt,

" I know how it may sound, I assure you, I have asked myself the same questions, but once we discovered that your planet had statistics that closely related to our own planet, our commander gave me no choice, I was forced into carrying out this expedition, and I had to choose my best men to accompany me. We had no idea what to expect, but if I had disobeyed a direct order from our commander… well, it doesn't bare thinking about what may have happened to us. We came here for research purposes, and it is our hope that you will assist us in our duty." replied Dr Stantham. Chiron seemed puzzled as he looked at each of the scientists one by one.

"It seems strange though Dr, that your commander would delegate such a mission without in depth prior research into our world, if you knew enough about this planet, you would have known that it is inhabited, would you not?

Thoughts raced through the Dr's head as he had himself once thought the same aboard the craft. The Dr looked up at Chiron now seeming reluctant to speak,

"I have myself thought about this, but I merely passed off the thoughts, as it could have merely shown that our commander trusts me and my team to carry out such an expedition!" Chiron then turned his attention to Professor Lockley,

"Did any of the rest of you not question what was being asked of you?" but professor Lockley didn't reply. He seemed lost in his own thoughts finally seeing the reality of what they were doing. Each of the scientists had begun having the same thoughts and they began to realise that they had maybe rushed into the expedition without questioning the commander. The Dr. soon broke the silence which had befallen the room,

"Everything you have said is true Chiron, having heard your comments it has made me realise that we may have acted a little rashly, and the reasons for the commanders sudden decisions are unknown, but I feel that there is more than enough cause for us to stay for a while longer on this planet. Whether or not we agree with our commanders decisions, we still need to fulfil our duty and our purpose for being here."

Chiron stood up and looked at the entire company of scientists,

"I did not mean to scare you gentlemen, but these questions had been racing through my mind ever since I first met you in the Teumessian forest. I still see that you are tired and I will have you rest in the chambers upstairs, we will wait and see what tomorrow brings. Alaya will you please show the gentlemen to their rooms."

"Thank you very much Chiron, I cannot stress enough the gratitude we have for your hospitality" replied Dr Stantham.

Chiron then exited the room and Alaya led the company out of the room and up the winding staircase which they had once noticed upon entering the house. As they reached the second floor, it was very similar to downstairs. There was yet another large corridor with various doors on either side and with walls adorned with painting and antiquities, the only difference was that at the far end of the hall there was a large panelled window overlooking the village below.

"There are three rooms down the end of the hall near the window which are ready for two occupants in each," said Alaya gently, Professor Cumbridge then turned to Alaya with his tired eyes,

"Thank you kind lady and good night to you,"

"Good night to you gentlemen," replied Alaya before then making her way back down stairs. The company of scientists made their way to end of the hall. Michael and Gordon entered one of the rooms, the Professor's John Cumbridge and Quinn

Lockley entered another and Étoile and Dr Stantham entered the last of the three rooms.

    As Dr Stantham entered his room he noticed two large king size four poster beds neatly made with silk sheets. There was also a large wooden cabinet and matching wardrobe occupying the room. On the right hand side of the doorway was a window which looked out over the village below and the neighbouring villages. Étoile removed his heavy space suit revealing his ordinary clothing beneath, and then headed for the bed on the left of the large room. The Dr however decided to go to the window after shutting the door. As he stood at the window he began to see more of the planet that surrounded him, and that even in the darkness there was much beauty to be seen. However, in the distance he could see one area of the planet that was darker than the rest. The dark shadowed land seemed to spread far and wide. It sent shivers down his spine as looked upon it, and for some unknown reason he felt sadness. Soon the Dr. moved away from the window and settled down in the strange bed for a night of uneasy sleep.

    The home of Chiron soon slept and all was quiet as everyone awaited the day that would soon follow. The Doctors dreams were filled with questions and tormenting images of the commander and the mission, whilst all the time his thoughts were overwhelmed by the feeling of regret.

8

The Overlords Sanctuary

"Good people do not need laws to tell them to act responsibly, while bad people will find a way around the laws."

Within the boundaries of the shadowed land, everywhere had become shrouded in darkness, a darkness accompanied by an eerie silence. The volcano that stood tall over the town poured streams of smoke from its mouth, however, the volcano was inactive, and had been for some time. Many years prior, the volcano had been transformed into a sanctuary for the overlord, one of the most evil beings that the world inhabited.

At the foot of the volcano there was a large piece of volcanic rock which was being used as a doorway. Two guards stood at the entrance dressed in black like the creature who once rode the ghost the horse. Akaz and his men neared the doorway and the guard moved the rock aside with little effort. Akaz marched his men through the doorway and into the enormous hollowed out volcanic mountain. Within the sanctuary of the overlord, all was silent and there was a damp and rotten smell filling what little air was available. Small pieces of rock fell from above and a never-ending darkness loomed over them. Trails of dried lava also adorned the walls like decorations and the ground was uneven and hot to the touch. There was also a legion of darkly clothed sinister looking men like the guards at the doorway. They walked around within the boundaries of the sanctuary. They shuffled across the rocky floors clutching large black staffs. Centralised within the sanctuary there was also a pool of lava sitting dormant, most likely the remnant lava of past volcanic activeness.

Akaz and the red soldiers stood near the pool of lava, with an orange gleam reflecting upon their faces. Steam rose upward toward them and caused beads of perspiration to drip from their brow. On the far side of the large chasm there was a unevenly carved, winding staircase which looked as if it had been formed out of the rock of the volcano. At the peak of the staircase there stood an old wooden doorway, Akaz was the first to notice the door slowly opening inward. Its hinges creaked and the wood cracked, and out from behind the door there stepped yet another darkly clad creature. However, he looked different, he was older than the others, and his spine was bent in the shape of an archway. He donned a long black robe and his face was unshielded and wrinkled with age; time hadn't been kind to him. He had long grey hair and he clutched a long and bent silver staff. He did however have one similarity to the other dark creatures, his eyes. They looked big and black, yet empty and cold. The crooked and weary creature was Malvo, the overlord of the shadowed land. It was he that had summoned Akaz.

Malvo made his way down the stone steps with slow progression, due to his old deteriorating body. Eventually he reached the foot of the stairway and began walking toward Akaz and the red soldier's .His black eyes pierced Akas' soul as he made his way toward him; although he was a frail old man he did not look kind, and an unprecedented evil dwelled within him. "I see you have returned home Akaz" said Malvo in a scratchy, stern and almost inaudible voice.

"I have my lord, and we bring good news with us!" replied Akaz in a quiet voice. Akaz seemed nervous and on edge as the old man continued to stare with his dark emotionless eyes.

"Good, do you have what I asked for?" Malvo continued,

"I do my lord, they arrived shortly before we did. We held back slightly in our craft so that we wouldn't be seen."

"What do you mean 'They'? I only required the one!" said Malvo returning a harsh reply,

"I know my lord… but the plan seemed more realistic to bring others along too, too much suspicion may have arisen otherwise" replied Akaz.

"I suppose… you have done well, at least now I have more to choose from!" said Malvo, "I trust the next stage of our plan is ready to proceed?" he continued with more severity,

"Yes, of course my lord, we are quite ready, although, I will also require the aid of your army and horses, so that we may execute the plan with more force. They landed in the Teumessian forest, so there is a high likely hood of them being with Chiron, he is the centaur who protects the forest" said Akaz. The old man stood leaning on his staff staring at Akaz.

"Do whatever it takes, and do it fast and efficiently. Ensure sure you bring me the healthiest and youngest of them, only then will my plan be enabled to reach the final stage!" said Malvo with a maniacal voice. "I also trust that those humans will cause us no trouble Akaz?" he continued,

"We have done everything you have asked of us my lord, the commander was under our control from the minute we landed on earth, your dark magic allowed us to put him in a deep trance, and your cleverness meant that we could get him to act upon our every word without those closest to him noticing something queer. We also had control over the scientist's computer systems making them think that they had discovered our planet by themselves."

"You have served me well, I never doubted you, however… it is not yet complete, you need waste no time in completing the next stage of the plan, I am not long from this world, bring me one of those scientists… by any means necessary!" Malvo concluded with a demonic glint in his eye.

9

Chirons Fate

"You don't develop courage by being happy in your relationships every day. You develop it by surviving difficult times and challenging adversity."

After awakening from a disturbed night of sleep, Dr. Stantham had once again returned to the window within his room. He stood and watched as the light of the planet was rekindled. There was no sunrise, the light just seemed to reappear as if someone had switched on a light. The Dr peered out of the condensation covered window pane watching as Valosia began to fill with many centaurs. Doors to homes began to open and what seemed to look like an old market in the near distance, had begun set up. There were wooden tables covered with fruit and vegetables and some were selling small carved stone and wooden toys. The Valosian realm emanated peace and the inhabitants were all part of one big family. Within the Dr's chambers Étoile was still sleeping. Soon though the call of Alaya awoke him as she invited the scientists downstairs for breakfast. However all the peace and niceties were unable to vanquish the feelings of regret in the doctor's mind. He had now also conjured some reluctance for facing the day ahead and more conversations which were inevitably going to take place with Chiron and Alaya.

"Are you alright?" Étoile asked his father, "it's just… you look a little saddened by something" he continued,

" I am fine son, I just have many thoughts and unanswered questions filling my mind that is all" replied the Dr, " I am also afraid of the future and its uncertainty" he added. Étoile looked at his father but didn't seem to share his father's worries,

"I personally don't think we have much to concern ourselves with… I mean, what have we got back home apart from ourselves and the Krupto initiative. We have no other family and neither do the other men, our lives revolve around studying the stars and the universe and other planets that surround us. So, correct me if I'm wrong, but are we not on another planet? We are living our dream and the people we have met thus far are turning out to be more like a family to us than anyone back on earth!" replied Étoile with a level of annoyance in his voice.

" I suppose you are right, I hadn't thought of it that way, I was too caught up in whether or not we have made the right decisions… you are a very bright young man, and as long as you are with me, well… I suppose I can call anywhere my home" replied the Dr with an emotional undertone. Their conversation was interrupter however, by the second call of Alaya reminding them of the breakfast that had been prepared for them. "Let's go, it sounds like we are wanted down stairs" said the Dr with a little grin and a quiet chuckle. They made their way downstairs to meet with the others. Having returned downstairs Étoile passed through the doorway and into the same room that they had eaten in the night before. The Dr followed closely behind and saw everyone already sitting and eating an array of different foods. Everyone had become rid of their spacesuits and they seemed comfortable as they indulged on bacon, eggs and different sized pastries. Michael and Gordon once again filled their mouths with food whilst Chiron sat at the head of the table with only a glass of water in his hand.

"Good morning gentlemen, please, sit and eat" said Chiron to Étoile and Dr Stantham as they entered the room.

"Thank you, I wasn't expecting all of this" replied the Dr with a smile on his face which highlighted his sudden change in mood.

When breakfast came to an end, a short goblin like creature entered the room, he wore a white stained shirt and large black boots. He wasn't very attractive but seemed kind and friendly to all that met him. He had large ears and a hairy chin and walked with a slight wobble because of his small stumpy legs. The creatures name was Bokin and he was the cook and servant for the house of Chiron.

"Have you finished your meal my masters?" said Bokin with a gruff and deep voice,

"Yes thank you Bokin, it was delicious" replied Chiron. Michael and Gordon stared at Bokin and their jaws dropped; they had never seen anything like him before and their puzzled expressions were seen by everyone in the room. Bokin himself also noticed the way they stared at him,

"Can I help you masters? Do I have something on my face?" Bokin said jokingly, Michael and Gordon grinned and turned away in embarrassment. Bokin walked around the table and cleared the plates, dishes and goblets of water until the table was free from clutter.

"The day is bright once again gentlemen, and I don't feel any need for us to stay in this house any longer, come with me and I will show you more of Valosia, the market is also starting to bustle, let us see if there is anything there that you would like" said Alaya as she invited the company to explore more of the realm.

"If you don't mind Alaya, I would like to stay here a while and talk with your father" said Dr Stantham,

"Of course Dr" said Alaya with a smile, before leaving the room with by Michael, Gordon, Étoile, Professor Cumbridge and Professor Lockley. Chiron and Dr Stantham soon found themselves sitting alone within the large dining room. The Dr stood up and moved to a seat closer to Chiron.

"I see you are in a better mood this morning Dr, I did not mean to upset you last night, but those questions and queries had plagued my mind since the moment I first met you" said Chiron.

"You were right to ask those questions Chiron, in fact it helped me and made me realise what a fool I had been to jump into this so hastily. I have always been a man who has studied the universe, and I more than anyone knew the risks of such an expedition but I never once questioned our commander." replied the Dr, " but this morning I had a conversation with my son, and he made me realise that coming here maybe wasn't such as bad decision. You and your daughter have made us feel more than welcome and you have begun to feel like close friends for us" the Dr. continued.

" I am happy that you feel this way, my home is very big and only me and my daughter live here since my wife passed away two years ago. Since you have arrived I have seen my daughter smile more than I have seen her smile in a very long while, so if you do wish to stay here Dr then you are more than welcome."

A feeling of relief and happiness began to overcome the Dr and he began to feel more at ease.

"I would like to ask you a question if you don't mind Chiron" said Dr Stantham,

"Of course Dr, what is it?,"

"Upon entering your realm, we noticed an inscription carved into the archway, and we saw the same inscription above the doorway of your home, I was just curious about what it meant."

"I see you have a very observational eye Dr," Chiron said with a smile, "it reads, *Valosia Valtakunta Rauhan Jakoti Tarnhelm,* which loosely translates in the common tongue as, 'The realm of peace, and the home of the Tarnhelm'" replied Chiron.

"What is the Tarnhelm?" the Dr. continued with intrigue.

"Instead of me telling you about the *'Tarnhelm'* I shall show you instead." continued Chiron.

"Oh… ok" said the Dr with confusion. Chiron then stood and made his way to the door,

"Follow me my friend!"

Chiron walked out of the dining room and into the main hall. He then headed for a small wooden door which had been placed under the main staircase, hidden from view. The Dr followed behind Chiron closely and watched as the large wooden door was opened following a spoken incantation. Chiron spoke aloud the word, "ELDOOMIEN,"

"Keep that to yourself my friend" said Chiron, the Dr smiled and nodded then watched as the door sprung open and allowed the darkness that lay within to seep out into the hall.

"Is that your language?" asked the Dr,

"No my friend, it is an ancient language that I picked up from books and legends, I needed a password for this door so that only I could enter, and I thought it suitable." replied Chiron,

"What does it mean?"

"Open!" chuckled Chiron as such an ancient word meant something so simple. Chiron proceeded to enter through the doorway, followed soon after by the Dr. They both entered into the dark and narrow passageway with the door behind them creaking to a close. Chiron began to whistle in a continuous high pitch sound and suddenly, candles began lighting up the passage. One by one the candles flickered with a tall flame giving enough light for the entirety of the surrounding area to be seen.

"Follow me Dr.," said Chiron before making his way down the narrow passageway. It seemed to go on forever and sloped downwards further into the ground at a steep incline. Chiron and the Dr made their way further and further down beneath Chiron's home.

"How far beneath your home will this take us?" asked the Dr,

"About 200 feet I think, I wanted my most treasured possessions to be kept safe away from anyone but myself and Alaya" replied Chiron. Soon the walking came to a halt as the golden glimmer of a carved heavy door was seen reflecting the light of the candles. "We are here Dr" said Chiron before reaching for a wooden box on the wall, he opened up the box and inside there was a large golden key. He picked it up and placed it into the key hole of the golden door. The Dr. once again noticed the word *'Tarnhelm'* had been engraved into the gold of the door along with leaves and the faces of Chiron and Alaya; it was a very decorative door, but it was what lay hidden beyond the door that interested the Dr.

With a heavy clunk and blast of age old dust, the door moved sideways disappearing into the dry dirt wall. The room within then became visible. It had been filled with many treasures and precious jewels, such as necklaces, bracelets, rings and earrings, all of which had been fashioned from gold, silver and other precious metals like platinum. Each of the pieces of jewellery had been encrusted with precious jewels, such as diamonds and rubies which each flickered as they reflected the candle light which surrounded the room. The jewels sat upon velvet cushions protected behind glass cabinets which had been locked. The room was vast, and the value of everything in it was too high to calculate. As the Dr. looked around the room with gold reflecting in his eyes, he noticed at the far end of the room there sat something that stood out from all of the other jewels.

"Each one of my most treasured possessions are contained within this one room, you can probably now appreciate why it is so far beneath my home. Over there is what we are here to see" said Chiron, although the Dr. already had a feeling that he knew what he was about to be taken to. Chiron walked across the room and headed toward a large glass box which had been edged with silver. The piece of treasure within sat upon yet another velvet cushion, and the glass box itself sat atop a white marble pedestal, which looked Greek in design. Within the glass box there laid a golden helmet. It had wings carved onto its sides, and two oval eye holes fluidly extended down into a long nose piece adorned with carved vines, small black garnet stones and ancient inscriptions. The helmet itself looked ancient, but also expertly crafted and something of immense beauty. Its polished surface allowed the Dr to see his own reflection. The Dr. was startled and taken from his awe inspired gaze as Chiron began to speak softly in his ear, "this is the Tarnhelm my friend" he then pointed at the helmet. The Dr. continued to stare at the helmet and he felt an unusual feeling residing within him, and it almost seemed as if the helmet was staring back.

"Why is it so special to you and your people?" asked the Dr,

"This helmet is an ancient piece of magical armour that was crafted by sorcerers, who had extraordinary powers in the days of old. It beholds an immense power that allows anyone who wears it to either change their form, or hide themselves completely, as it can act as a cloak of invisibility. It may not have as many jewels as other pieces of treasure in this room may have, but the power it has is far beyond anything else I know of" replied Chiron,

"How did you come to own such an item?" continued the Dr.

" I am not too sure, all I know is that one of my ancestors from many years ago won the helmet in a battle against a powerful wizard, it was most likely the wizard who created the helmet. It was this same ancestor who had this home made in this part of the world, which I have now acquired along with all the jewels in this room as well as the Tarnhelm. I feel that my ancestor was proud of this battle which may be the reason why he included the name of this helmet in the title of our village" replied

Chiron. The Dr continued to look at the Tarnhelm and then turned and looked at all the other treasures once again.

"I am truly honoured to have been shown this, but you had better watch out for dragons. Having all this treasure stashed away beneath your home could draw their attention!" remarked the Dr jokingly , however Chiron did not laugh back as he did not see it as a joke. "What… are you telling me there are actually dragons in this world too?" continued the doctor.

"Yes my friend… and they have attempted to steal this treasure before many years ago, which is why it is now locked away down here, out of their reach" replied Chiron. The Dr's eyes grew larger and he swallowed the lump that had made its way into his throat.

"I suppose anything is possible here though isn't" said the Dr.

" I hope I can trust you Dr, and that I can have confidence in knowing you will not tell another living soul of this room, not even your own son, as I have shown you this to give you comfort in knowing I am now your friend and that you can trust me" said Chiron in a kind soft voice.

The Distant Glimmer

" Of course my friend, I will honour your privacy and will tell no one" replied the Dr seeming to now feel as though he had found a good friend in Chiron even though he hadn't known him that long. Chiron and Dr Stantham stood silently surrounded by the many treasures, and the Dr looked, still, at the beauty of the Tarnhelm noticing its every detail, he also noticed that the helmet was very large.

"It's very big isn't it!" said the Dr as he broke the silence in the room,

"Excuse me!" said Chiron seeming baffled by the Dr's query,

"The Tarnhelm… it looks very big, who was it made for?" replied the Dr

"Oh… yes," giggled Chiron, "another of its powers is that it can adjust its size to match the wearer, and it stays the size of the head of the last person to wear it, and in this case it would have been my ancestor, he was a very large centaur with a very big head, in all senses of the phrase" Chiron continued followed by yet another laugh.

"So if I were to wear it, the Tarnhelm would adjust its size to fit my head?" asked the Dr

"Yes, certainly" replied Chiron

"It is truly amazing?" said the Dr in a voice that displayed his amazement.

As the Dr continued to look at the Tarnhelm he began to notice that it was shaking slightly. He turned and looked at some of the other treasures in the room, and noticed that they too were shaking and trembling. " Look Chiron, your possessions are moving" said the Dr in an anxious voice,

"Yes I noticed that myself, I also thought I heard something from above… something loud" replied Chiron. The two of them began to express worry and panic, then from the distance there came the voice of Alaya shouting down the passageway to her father.

"Father… come quickly, come quickly we need your help!" shouted Alaya, seeming scared and speaking with desperation in her voice. As Chiron heard his daughters cries he ran from the room followed by the Dr, and locked the golden door, before sprinting up the passageway. Soon Alaya could be seen standing at the top of the passage way holding open the wooden door under the stairs,

"What is it Alaya?" yelled Chiron still with panic in his voice,

THE DISTANT GLIMMER

"We are under attack father, the outer walls of our village are being destroyed, I came inside with the others as soon as I saw what was happening!" replied Alaya. Chiron and the Dr then left the passage way closing the wooden door behind them. Everyone stood in the main hallway of Chiron's home, whilst loud noises came from outside along with the screams of younglings and female centaurs.

"Alaya, you and the gentlemen hide yourselves, get to safety" said Chiron,

"No father I want to come with you!" said Alaya with tears running down her face,

"Please! get the men to safety, look after them I do not want you involved in this… GO!" said Chiron in a commanding voice. Alaya and the scientists ran upstairs. Chiron made his way to a door which stood opposite the dining room, he opened it up and inside were a selection of various different weapons from swords to bows and arrows. Chiron entered the room and picked up a large black bow and a quiver filled with red tipped arrows which he strapped over his shoulders. He left the room and made his way outside where he saw many of his own army frantically trying to hold off the enemy who had now successfully destroyed the outer wall that once stood around the perimeters of Valosia. The archway had also been destroyed. " Get yourselves to safety… all of you!" shouted Chiron trying to alert all of the women and children of the village to get out of sight and to a safer place. As he stood, enormous fire balls began to fly overhead destroying anything that they came into contact with, such as homes and the marble paths that once looked so pristine. The market had also been destroyed leaving only piles of rubble and dirt in its wake. Chiron looked at the wall that had been destroyed and noticed men making their way into Valosian territory. They were all clad in black robes with hoods hiding their faces. They each clutched staffs which acted as weapons. Bolts of lightning were emitted from the ends, which killed anyone that they struck. Chiron couldn't believe his eyes, he reached for his arrows and placed one in his bow, and he pulled it and released it causing it to cut through the damp morning air. The arrow pierced the flesh of one of the black eyed beings, but it was only one death, and many more of the dark creatures were still entering into Chiron's village. Centaurs raged on with their swords and their arrows trying to kill as many of the dark creatures as possible. Chiron heard a loud screeching sound from above his head, he looked up and noticed six jet black winged horses with fire in their eyes, it was Akaz and his men riding into the battle from above. The screeching was the sound the horses made as the men pulled at their reins. Akaz made eye contact with Chiron and expressed an evil grimace. Akaz decreased the altitude at which the horse was flying before reaching for a staff of his own. He aimed it at Chiron and a bright red bolt of lightning spread across the sky and made its way to Chiron. It hit him full force and caused him to collapse to the floor. Chiron lay on his side unable to move and his bow was knocked from his grasp and rolled five feet from his reach. He lay shaking uncontrollably watching as the battle continued around him, with many of Chiron's own army meeting their demise. Akaz and his men touched down on the floor close to Chiron whilst still sitting upon their horses.

"Strange time to take a nap isn't it centaur" said Akaz to Chiron before letting out a sarcastic chuckle. Akaz dismounted his horse and made his way to Chiron's home. Within his mind Chiron was shouting, but could not seem to let out what he felt in words. The red soldiers surrounded Chiron and prevented anyone from getting to the house leaving Akaz enough time to break in and take what he was looking for. Fire balls continued to fly overhead and destroy Valosia, and screams could still be heard as the battle showed no signs of stopping.

Akaz sniffed the air as he walked through the debris filled hallway of Chiron's home. He could sense the fear of Alaya and the scientists, and he followed the scent and made his way upstairs. Still sniffing the air and clutching his staff he headed for a hatch in the ceiling. He stood beneath it and then blew open the door with his magic. A hole opened up the ceiling and within it, Akaz saw Alaya and the scientists. The heart rates of each of the scientists began to rise, and Alaya stepped forth and looked down at Akaz.

"What do you want? Leave us alone!" said Alaya with a nervous, and shaky voice,

" I am afraid I cannot do that beast, I have come here for something and I will not leave without it" replied Akaz. Dr Stantham began to have many thoughts racing through his head and he started to think of the Tarnhelm. His initial thought was that maybe Akaz was trying to steal the treasure. However before the Dr had the chance to say anything Akaz began an incantation. Another bolt of lightning flew through the air. It locked onto Étoile and began pulling him through the air as if he had been trapped within a floating bubble.

The Dr tried to grab him to pull him back but he did not succeed.

"NO, give him back… give him back!" shouted the Dr trying his best to get his son. Alaya also leaped forward and tried to reach him, but she missed and fell through the hole in the ceiling and landed on the floor below. Akaz then let out a loud whistle. Étoile was under his power and had fear in his eyes. He tried to break free from the grasp but Akaz knocked him unconscious with yet another incantation.

" NO, give me back my son!" said the Dr in desperation as he tried once more to get his son back with one final leap forth from the hole in the ceiling. However, as the Dr. leapt through the air a ghost horse smashed through the window at the end of the upstairs hallway. Akaz made his way to the horse and Dr Stantham chased after him as he tried to grab his son, but once again he failed to reach him. Akaz flew off on the horse and signalled for his men to join him. Chiron still lay dormant on the ground and the Dr. noticed him from the window of the second floor. The Dr. alerted the others and ran downstairs to help him. Akaz concurrently called the black eyed beings away from the battle and he and his men flew off on their ghostly destrier's and headed back towards the shadowed land of Murdreddia, with Étoile unconscious on the back of Akas' horse.

Dr Stantham ran across the cracked marble and rubble and knelt down beside Chiron, whose life was draining from him with each passing second. Alaya soon came running toward her father crying and shouting due to understandable upset. Alaya saw her injured father lying on the floor incapable of moving. She got as close as possible and tried to comfort him in his final moments. Chiron had a tear running down his face, and he tried to speak with what little energy he had left.

"I love you Alaya, and I am sorry I could not win this battle, and that you were exposed to such risk. Dr., my friend, please promise me you will take care of my daughter,"

"Of course Chiron" replied the Dr. with his own emotional state overpowering his ability to speak clearly.

"Dr… take the Tarnhelm… go to Eldrador… and seek out Aldrien… get, your son back!" Chiron then slowly faded away and he breathed his final breath before passing away on the rubble and blood filled marble ground of Valosia.

THE DISTANT GLIMMER

Alaya sobbed and her tears could not be contained. Sadness had overcome everyone, Michael and Gordon looked around at Valosia and noticed its beauty had disappeared. Women and children once again came outside to search for their loved ones among the many who had lost their lives in the battle. It was not an image one would want to keep in their minds forever. Dr Stantham moved across to Alaya and tried his best to comfort her even though he himself was worrying about his own son. The two of them knelt next to the body of the bravest centaur they had ever known…Chiron.

The Orbis Chronicles

10

Company of Ten

"Courage is better than keenest steel."

Two emotional days came to pass in Valosia. Chiron had been buried near the waterfall which stood overlooking the entire village behind Chiron's home, and everyone mourned his passing, especially his daughter Alaya. Many centaur guards and some of the female centaurs tried their best to clear up the aftermath of the battle between the Valosians and the Murdreddians. Rubble and blood could be seen in every direction, and only the sounds of rocks being cleared away and brushes sweeping along the floor could be heard. The air was damp and lay heavy with a fog and drizzle fell from the sky onto the blood stained marble floor. Valosia had lost its beauty and now looked like a completely different realm. Within the home of Chiron, Alaya and the scientists sat in a large living room near a log fire which flickered and crackled and emitted a warming golden glow around the room. Alaya didn't look as happy as she once did which was understandable, and the scientists themselves were in a saddened mood. The Dr was the first to speak on that morning, " I feel all of this has been our fault, if only we hadn't of come here none of this would of happened, I would still have my son and Chiron would be alive and well to this day" the professors agreed with the Dr., but Alaya frowned and seemed disapproving of his words.

"Do not blame yourself Dr, you were not to know that the events that have taken place would of come to pass in such a devastating way. We centaurs have known for many years about the presence of the black eyed beings not too far from here, but they have never once attempted to come near us, let alone attack us, no one was to know about any of this"

"I haven't really said a lot since we arrived but I too feel that this expedition has been a mistake, we have all rushed into this so hastily and now we cannot leave as one of our friends has been taken from us. However, no matter how we feel, we need to do all we can to get him back" said Michael in a calm yet stern voice.

"He's right Bernard, we need to get your son back, we cannot sit around here feeling sorry for ourselves!" said Professor Lockley to Dr Stantham. Everyone agreed with Professor Lockley and Alaya nodded and turned back to Dr Stantham,

"What did my father say to you in his final words Dr?"

"He said that I must take the Tarnhelm and travel to Eldrador in order to find someone called Aldrien, but I don't know what the latter half of it meant!" replied the Dr.

"The Tarnhelm, how do you know about that?" said Alaya seeming quite perturbed.

"When you went with the others to the market your father showed me the room with his most treasured possessions, and he showed me the Tarnhelm. He told me about how it came to be here, I think he showed it to me so that we could put our trust in one other" said the Dr.

"I see… well it seems that my father wants you to have it, and have it you will as I must acquiesce to his final request," replied Alaya.

"But what is Eldrador and who is Aldrien?" asked Professor Lockley with curiosity.

"Eldrador is another realm about a day's walk away from here. It is the realm of the witches!" said Alaya. Shock seemed to spread across the faces of the scientists as their preconceived vision of an atypical witch was not a nice one.

"Do not worry gentlemen, they would mean us no harm, we centaurs often visit the witches and we are very good friends with them. In fact they are one of the very few races of people who we can truly trust in this world. One of the witches whom we trust the most is Aldrien, whom my father spoke of in his final moments. Unlike many of the other witches she sees all, she knows of everyone on this planet. She sees their past, their present and can also see glimpse of their future, as she is the soothsayer of this world!" said Alaya trying to make sense of her father's final words.

"So Chiron wanted us to seek her help?" said Michael as he began to make sense of the situation,

"It seems so!" replied Alaya.

"Then we must go there as soon as possible, Aldrien can help us on our quest to get my son back!" said Dr Stantham trying to encourage the others to help him find Étoile.

"We must first get you the Tarnhelm Dr, as my father must have known that it may be of some help to you on this quest. I feel that he also knew that there is far darker plan at work here than just a kidnapping!" said Alaya with seriousness.

The conversation ended and the room cleared. The scientists began collecting supplies for the journey to Eldrador. Alaya and the Dr disappeared down the passageway in order to retrieve the Tarnhelm from its glass case, and Michael and Gordon assisted Bokin with the preparation of food and drink. Professor Lockley and Professor Cumbridge had begun searching all the rooms of the house collecting weapons which they had either never used or seen before. They also discovered some pieces of armour which would protect them against any attacks. Everything they found was gathered up into black leather satchels that Alaya had provided them with.

    The day continued with slow progression and rain continued to fall from the gods. Alaya and the Dr. re-joined with the others, and Dr Stantham now wore a back pack which had been crafted from a strong green velvet material. Inside the pack was the most precious piece of armour that the entire Valosian village had come to own, the Tarnhelm. It was going to be Dr Statham's responsibility to keep it safe.

"I see you found the weaponry then gentlemen!" said Alaya to the Professors.

"Yes, but the armour we found, although it looks very well crafted I feel it may be too big for us!" replied Professor Cumbridge,

"Do not worry gentlemen, I think we may have some smaller pieces of armour that you can borrow, we have some that was crafted for the youngsters that maybe the perfect size for you." said Alaya. "Those swords you have found were my fathers, many a battle were fought with those when he was in the prime of his life. He was very much the master swordsman when he was younger, I also used to practice with one of those swords when I was about ten years old" said Alaya as she reflected on her and her father's youth with a tear in her eye and with a heavy heart filled with emotion.

"I am sorry if we have upset you Alaya, I didn't realise there would be so many memories left behind in swords" said Professor Lockley as he tried to comfort the grieving Alaya.

"It isn't your fault, there are memories attached to everything in this house" replied Alaya. Everyone stood in the main hallway clutching satchels and weapons and food as the light of the planet once again vanished and darkness filled its place.

"It is again time for some rest gentlemen, we will need to be up early tomorrow in order to get a head start on the day, I hope to reach Eldrador by the end of tomorrow" said Alaya. "I bid you goodnight gentlemen" she continued before making her way upstairs to her chambers.

"We too should go and get some rest as I feel we have a long day ahead of us" said Dr Stantham to the other scientists, even though he himself knew he wouldn't be able to sleep because of the thoughts of his son. Everyone made their way to their rooms to sleep through the night awaiting the arrival of the long day that was to follow.

***

Morning once again soon arrived bright and clear with the dampness and the drizzle a distant memory of the day before. The night had seemed to disappear in no time and it was now the first day of the quest to get Étoile back.

"It is time to wake gentlemen, we have a long day ahead of us" shouted Alaya as she woke the scientists from their slumber. Tired looking faces emerged from the rooms, Michael and Gordon seemed ready to fall asleep on anything they stood near, "your armour is ready for you in the main hallway and Bokin has put each of your satchels ready along with your food, drink and weaponry. We will also be joined on our journey by four of my fathers most trusted guardsmen, they too await you downstairs!" said Alaya before making her way back down the winding staircase at the end of the hall.

As they eventually reached the foot of the stairs they saw the halls tables laden with the armour and weapons, they also noticed Bokin standing ready to give the scientists their satchels. "Gentlemen, let me introduce you to my friends who will accustom us on our journey," said Alaya. Just then, through the main door of the house stepped four very tall and muscular centaurs. Each of them had long flowing black and brown hair that rested on their silky furred backs. Neatly trimmed beards also highlighted their strong jaw lines. Alaya pointed to the centaur on the far left to begin introducing them to the scientists,

"This is my fathers most trusted and oldest friend, he has seen many battles and has always been at my father's side, his name is Pholus," she then continued to point at the next centaur in the line "next to Pholus you will see Elatus, another of my father's dearest friends and an expert in battle" she then turned to the final two centaurs "and the two on my right are Bienor and Nessus, again they are experts in battle and are regarded as two of the best guardsmen in Valosia," the centaurs and scientists greeted one another and Alaya soon announced the urgency to leave the home. "Gentlemen, we must be leaving soon, collect your belongings from the table and your satchels from Bokin and meet me and the guardsmen outside the house." She then turned and exited the house along with the four centaurs leaving the scientists to prepare themselves for the journey that lay ahead.

The scientists were soon ready and they rejoined Alaya and the centaurs outside the home of Chiron under the morning light of the planet. The day looked to be dry and clear and the air smelled clean; Valosia also looked cleaner and was beginning to return back to its original beauty with much of the rubble and blood having been cleared away. The day was starting off well and there was now a company of ten who were ready for the quest to Eldrador, five centaurs and five scientists. Bokin bid them all farewell before closing the door of the house.

The Distant Glimmer

"Come my friends, we must begin our journey" said Alaya having nominated herself to lead the way to Eldrador. The centaurs and the scientists followed her closely and they made their way out of the boundaries of Valosia, over the crumbling and damaged wall of the realms boundaries. It was from there that the quest finally began.

II

Eldrader

***

"You have done well Akaz!" said the creaky old voice of Malvo as he entered a dark and eerie room beneath the volcano. Dust filled the air and the smell of rock and the scent of something being burnt attacked the sinuses. Malvo appeared from the darkness and the light of candles which had been placed around the small room reflected upon his old wrinkled face. The light caught his face in such a way that it made him look even more evil and stern than usual. Around the outer edges of the small room which had been carved out beneath the volcano were Akaz and the red soldiers. The room was extremely hot and sweat poured from every orifice of their bodies, but there was a heart wrenching reason why they were in that room. In the centre of them all stood a tall metal board. It looked like a metal bed standing upright, and fixed to it was a tired and beaten Étoile. He was covered in dirt and dry blood, and he had chains attached to his arms and feet making it impossible for him to move. His shirt had been ripped slightly and his clothes were covered in dark marks which made it look as if he had been dragged across the ground. His hair was a mess and he was covered in sweat as he had been in the room for over twelve hours. Étoile looked up taking all his energy and strength to lift his head whilst still feeling the effects of the magic which Akaz had used. As he looked up, he saw the old man looking down on him with his dark and empty eyes.

"What do you want with me?" said Étoile in a whisper,. Malvo raised his hand and hit Étoile causing his brow to bleed.

"I ask the questions around here human!" said Malvo as he enforced his voice of authority. Étoile looked at the floor trying to hide the pain he now felt on the right side of his face.

"We leave tomorrow, be ready and waiting for my arrival at the main entrance as soon as the planets light is rekindled, and make sure the human male is chained tightly, I cannot have him escaping!" demanded Malvo in a strict voice.

"Do we tell the human of our plans sir?" Akaz asked Malvo,

"Do what you want with him, he won't be able to do anything with the information you give him, in fact, by the end of the week, he won't be doing much of anything!" Malvo replied before leaving the small room.

"What does he want with me?" Étoile asked with desperation.

"You're going to be going on a little journey tomorrow human, the overlord needs your life!" replied Akaz.

"What do you mean my life?" said Étoile with more nervousness.

"You'll find out soon enough!" replied Akaz. Étoile began to shake with terror, and the pupils of his eyes dilated with the fear at what he was being told.

"Why are your eyes not like the others? You look like a human yourself" Étoile asked Akaz.

"We are not from this realm. We are from another part of this world, but we were cast aside and treated with no respect from our own kind. One day we were out doing our duties for our old king, such as collecting herbs and fruits, when a man with huge black eyes came to us and offered us a proposition we could not refuse. He was offering us freedom and riches beyond our wildest dreams and we would not be slaves to our own kind any more. But if we are to get what he promised us, we must help him first, that is why you are here human, our knowledge of his plan is limited, all know is that when it is complete we will be rich and free from any bonds!" said Akaz. Etoile then glanced up at Akaz,

"You really trust this old man? What if he isn't telling you the truth?"

"Silence human! I will not here this insolence, he is the only one to have ever shown us kindness and any hope of a better future" replied Akaz before lifting his staff and once again forcing Étoile into an unconscious state.

***

As Dr Stantham walked with the company, he had thoughts and prayers in his mind for his son. He walked across the rocky uneven terrain of the planet's surface with the weight of the Tarnhelm bearing down on his back. Alongside him were the four professors and the five centaurs, all of whom were now wearing their armour which had been expertly crafted; it was silver with golden leaves embedded into various parts of the armours surface along with inscriptions in gold that read 'Valosia'. Everyone's armour was the same to show that they were all part of the same company. On the chest plates of the armour was an image of the Valosian coat of arms which had two centaurs standing side on facing each other with swords thrust into the air. There was also an inscription of an unknown language running around its edges. They were aesthetically pleasing piece of craftsmanship. As they traversed the terrain with their satchels over their shoulders the light of the planet was very bright. The stars beyond the atmosphere could still be seen along with many purple swirls and other distant planets. The surrounding area embraced natural tranquillity, and there were many sparkling trees and shrubs and high peaked mountains. There were also many gentle streams of crystal blue ice cold water. The planet was natural, untouched and peaceful.

"Why is your planet so uneven and rocky like this Alaya? And why is it everything sparkles with such beauty?" asked Michael.

The Distant Glimmer

"That is a good question Michael, I am no expert, but what I do know is what my father once told me. It has been known that a law of this planet has been in place for many centuries, we know not the reason why, but it is known that it is forbidden for the outer world to be changed. Every race on the planet has its own realm, and individual civilisations. The outer world is the planet's surface that stretches beyond the boundaries of the realms. Within the boundaries of a realm, a civilisation is able to do whatever they wish to the land they own, such as carve out paths and build houses, just like Valosia with its marble floors and white stone houses. Eldrador has also created its own unique land as you will soon see, but the terrain outside of these realms must not be touched. This is why everywhere looks so beautiful and natural, and is also the reason for the sparkle that the planet has, everywhere is naturally formed from precious stones, such as diamonds, these precious minerals reflect the planets light." Alaya replied.

"But why doesn't anyone touch the precious stones, what is stopping them from doing so, on earth diamonds and rubies are very rare and a lot of money is paid for someone to own them," asked Gordon.

"It is also known that part of the legend and law of this planet is that anyone who attempts to change the natural state of the planet, would be cursed for doing so, we do not know if this is true or not, but nobody has ever been brave enough to test it as of yet" replied Alaya.

The company continued to walk. They had been walking without rest now for around ten hours and everywhere had been so quiet and tranquil since they had begun their journey, with no signs of life to be seen anywhere. During their journey they had passed other realms which were home to different races such as Gigantria the home of the giants and Drakontos the home of the dragons with its thick forestry and damp environment. However, they too seemed quiet as if the planet had been engulfed by some kind of dark magic and unnatural silence.

The company stopped once on their journey to take a break and eat the food that Bokin, Michael and Gordon had prepared before the journey. They sat high up on a hill overlooking many of the realms beneath them. In the distance they saw Eldrador, a small realm, shrouded by trees, and lying dormant in the shadows of a gargantuan mountain, which stretched into an far reaching mountain range.

By now the armour that the company wore was beginning to feel heavy and began weighing them down causing their backs to ache and their legs to become weaker. Their satchels became empty and the food and drink had all gone. It was only Dr Stantham who had something heavy to carry. Soon though, there tired eyes had something to look upon, something that they had been waiting for since the journey began at the beginning of the day; Eldrador was in their sights,

"Here we are, ahead of you is the ancient realm of Eldrador" said Alaya as she brought everyone's attention to the dark uninviting realm ahead of them. The realm looked old and its surrounding walls were made from old dark wood, and its entrance was an enormous metal gate topped with what looked like arrow tips. The gate looked rusty and seemed to have been standing for many years.

"So far it seems my preconceptions of witches are going to become a reality, this doesn't look very welcoming!" said Professor Lockley as he seemed to begin having thoughts of panic and terror.

"I had to make you think it was going to be a nice place, or you would never have come, they are witches gentlemen, not fairies!" said Alaya as she admitted she had made the village sound more welcoming than it actually was. The scientists swallowed lumps that had come up into their throats.

"We cannot stand around here too long Alaya, we do not know what creatures surround us!" said Pholus in a quiet and concerned voice. Alaya agreed with Pholus and she led the way to the main gates in order to try and gain access to the village that lay within.

Alaya was the first to reach the gates and she could see the witches within patrolling the surrounding area dressed in dark attire. As she stood staring in at what was to greet them behind the gates, an old lady appeared from around a dark corner and came face to face with Alaya with the large gate standing between them. She wore a large black hat which left her eyes shadowed from the light, she was dressed all in black and her nails looked long and creepily sharp. She wasn't a very large lady but she seemed to have been given the role of gatekeeper, and was to be the one to decide whether or not the company would be allowed into Eldrador.

The Distant Glimmer

"Hello Rosina, it is I, Alaya, daughter of Chiron, the leader of the centaurs!" said Alaya has she greeted the old witch. Rosina looked up at Alaya and began expressing a familiarisation with whom she was looking upon. In a quiet and soft voice she said,

"Goodness, is it really you? My you have grown since last we met; I see you have come with Pholus"

"Hello Rosina good to see you again" replied Pholus as he too greeted the witch at the gate.

"But I do not recognize any of the others you have arrived with, especially those strange looking men with the unfamiliar garments" Rosina said as she pointed one of her crooked fingers in the direction of Dr Stantham.

"These are friends of mine and the other centaurs are trusted guards of my father," said Alaya as she tried her best to get everyone granted access into Eldrador.

"How is your father Alaya, I have not seen him in many years?" said Rosina softly,

"I am afraid it is not good news, this is why I have come to you today, we were involved in battle only days ago, and unfortunately my father was one of those who did not see its end" replied Alaya as she tried to hide the pain she felt within.

"I am sorry to hear that young one, but why are you here at Eldrador?" asked Rosina,

"One of my human friends here had his son taken from him during the battle. We have come here on a quest to try and get him back, and we thought Aldrien and her wisdom could help us on our quest" replied Alaya.

"I am sure she would help you Alaya, but I am afraid we too have some bad news, we were ambushed by the mountain trolls of Mount Malevolence nearly a week ago, and I am afraid they took Aldrien, it seemed the only reason for the ambush was so that they could kidnap her!" said Rosina in an tone of upset.

"Mount Malevolence, that doesn't sound very nice!" said Gordon as he tried to express his worriment.

"I don't believe it, why would they do something like this, mountain trolls are usually only concerned about what they will be eating next" said Pholus with concern.

THE DISTANT GLIMMER

"Have you tried to get her back?" asked Michael as he now grew concerned about the fate of Aldrien,

"Of course not dear boy, we witches wouldn't dare test the might of the mountain trolls, they can be very dangerous and even with our magic I feel we would be putting our lives at risk" said Rosina harshly. Everyone was in shock regarding what they were being told and they knew that the fate of the quest which they had begun relied on the help of Aldrien and her soothsaying abilities.

"We must get her back, no matter what dangers lay within those mountains!" said Alaya as she began showing her bravery. A trait that resided within her that had been passed down from her father.

"Are you sure that is wise, none of you have enough strength or power to defeat those trolls!" said Rosina as she tried to deter Alaya from the idea of getting Aldrien back.

"We have not magic nor power, but what we do have is the determination and strength which we create through friendship and hope, we must try and get her back as we, unlike you, have not given up hope!" said Alaya proudly. "We will go to

Mount Malevolence and bring Aldrien back to Eldrador no matter what state she is in!" Alaya continued.

"It is our only hope of getting my son back, I will join you no matter what, Alaya!" said Dr Stantham. Everyone else also agreed that they would go to the mountains even if they were terrified at the prospect of what they would find, and also of the probable prospect of them not coming out alive.

"Good luck my friends, I hope you return safely, here Alaya, take this!" said Rosina as she reached her hand through the gates and gave Alaya her wand, a long piece of smoothly carved old oak wood, " I know you do not know any spells but this wand will do whatever you think of in your mind, I gave my wand this charm as I kept forgetting my spells as I got older" continued Rosina,

"Thank you," replied Alaya with a hint of dismay in her words.

The company made their way toward the enormous mountain which stood in all its gloominess not too far away from Eldrador. The mountain stood high piercing the clouds that drifted across the sky in front of the stars that

The Distant Glimmer

flickered out yonder. It stood amidst many trees and a blanket of mist, awaiting the arrival of the company of ten who now held onto the hope that Aldrien was still alive.

The Orbis Chronicles

12

The Trolls of Mount Malevolence

Mount Malevolence stood proudly with a majestic grandeur. It towered over the many other mountains which it had been formed alongside. The mountain range seemed to go on for miles and all the mountains together seemed to act as a long wall blocking the path for anyone who wanted to get to the other side. The path up to Mount Malevolence was not an easy one; it required climbing over rocks and boulders and trudging through sharp brambles which had grown on the mountain side, along with other bushes that had thorns on their stems protecting a multitude of brightly coloured flowers from passers-by. From the mountain side Eldrador could still be seen, significantly darker than its surrounding areas with many trees occupying the majority of the realms land.

The Distant Glimmer

"I don't believe I am doing this!" exclaimed Professor Cumbridge seeming to have had the realisation of what he was doing invade his thought processes.

"What do you mean?" replied Dr Stantham

"Well look around you, we are walking up the side of an enormous mountain heading towards the habitat of mountain trolls to save a witch who we do not know, we are walking alongside centaurs, and to top it all off we are now on a quest to get your kidnapped son back from strange people with magical staffs and enormous soul piercing black eyes… who at any moment could turn up and kill us all!" replied a breathless and upset Professor Cumbridge.

"Do you think any of us wanted this to happen? We were all unsuspecting scientists who came here to research an unknown planet, none of this was planned, not by us at least!" said Dr Stantham with a loud assertive tone.

"I am sorry Bernard, it is all just getting a little too much, I was never ready for something like this" said Professor Cumbridge having noticed that Dr Stantham was upset.

"We have come so far gentlemen; we must complete this quest so that we can get Étoile back and try and return to some kind of normalisation" said Alaya trying to reassure the company and get their minds back on the task at hand.

The entrance to the mountain was clearly visible. The doorway had been carved into the mountain side and polished into a smooth gleaming grey stone. The outer edge of the doorway was glowing blue with an italic inscription, it read; *'This is the passage to the trolls of the mountain, knock on this door and you had better start counting, as fear is the emotion you will soon start to feel, and the trolls of the mountain will collect their next meal.'*

"That does not sound good, we cannot go through that doorway!" said Professor Cumbridge shaking and backing away.

"We have no other choice, we need to get through here and rescue Aldrien!" replied Alaya with assertion.

"But how do we get in, we don't just knock on the door that's for certain, that inscription has been carved into this entrance for a reason, these trolls obviously don't like strangers" said Professor Lockley with concern.

THE DISTANT GLIMMER

"The wand" said Alaya reaching for her satchel. She put her hand in and pulled out the wooden wand that Rosina had given her, "Rosina said that this wand doesn't need spells, I just have to think of something and the wand will do it," Alaya then proceeded to raise the wand and aim it towards the doorway. She closed her eyes to get a clearer picture of what she wanted the wand to do, and upon opening her eyes she noticed a flash of light cut through the air and make its way towards the doorway. The light covered the door and imbedded itself around its frame, and just then a blindingly white light shone outward lighting up the faces of everyone in the company. The door began to creak and move slightly until eventually it opened inward causing a blast of dust to fly into their faces. The door continued moving inward before sliding to the left and disappearing into the mountain side. The open doorway revealed an enormous dark chasm within. Alaya was the first to enter, her bravery had overcome her fear. The others soon followed after her and they noticed the enormity of the mountains hall. Many wooden beams ran across the carved ceiling which had been carved out of the rock of the mountain. Large boulders lay along the sides of the walls and strange shapes and mural's had been etched into the stone along with ancient inscriptions of an unknown language. There was very little natural light and the end of the hall could not be seen from where the company stood. Alaya used the wand again to create a source of light, although it made little difference to the amount they could see.

    "Let's walk further in, I feel we will not find Aldrien at the mountains entrance" said Alaya prompting the rest of the company to move forth deeper into the mountain. The darkness grew deeper, and the hall went on as far as the eye could wander. As of yet there had been no change in decoration. There were the same rocks and inscriptions on either side of the hall and the brittle beams and the mountain stone lay overhead. Soon though, however, Pholus heard sounds coming from the distance as he used his expert sense of hearing to pick out the faintest of audible noises.

    "I hear talking further down this hall, we must be quiet if we are not to be found!" said Pholus as he alerted the others to what he had begun hearing. Soon the others could hear the groaning deep voices of what had to be mountain trolls. A loud slap was also heard followed by the whine of a female,

The Distant Glimmer

"Aldrien!" said Michael with a tone of fear in his voice following a sharp intake of breath. Alaya looked at Michael and then looked to Pholus showing that she too thought the screams and cries from the distance were those of Aldrien.

"Quickly we must go to her, she could be in danger, be sure to stay quiet!" said Alaya before leading the company down the hallway. They picked up their speed whilst trying not put their feet down too heavy with each stride. Eventually they could see a light seeping out from another doorway to the left of the hallway. No other light could be seen and the hallway was pitch black and still seemed to go on for a few miles more. The cries of the female within the room grew louder than ever and it had become quite clear that she was in the room the company stood near.

"How do we get in there and get her out with those trolls killing us? We don't even know how many are in that room and whether or not the female we hear is Aldrien!" said Elatus who felt the need for voicing his concern.

"I may be able to help!" said Dr Stantham as he took the back pack off his shoulders,

"Of course, the Tarnhelm" whispered Alaya. The Dr knelt on the ground and opened up the back pack. He reached in and pulled out the golden helmet as gently as he could, and as it came out inch by inch it still looked perfect and untouched, and gleamed under the glow of Alaya's wand.

" I can put this on and look inside the room to see what we are dealing with" said the Dr. The others agreed it was their only option. The Dr grasped the Tarnhelm and brought it up to his head, he then put it on and it covered his eyes, it was far too big for him and it caused Gordon to chuckle slightly at the humorous sight before him. However, to Gordon's surprise the helmet began magically adjusting its size, each of its proportions became smaller, and it soon became the perfect fit for Dr Statham's cranium. Gordon stopped smiling and now shock had greeted his face. He looked on as he saw Dr Stantham slowly fading out of sight and becoming invisible to the eye.

"Can you still hear me?" whispered the Dr as he tried to make sure that the helmet didn't also disguise his voice,

"Yes we can hear you fine Dr" replied Alaya,

"I am moving to the doorway now" said the Dr as he tried to keep the others informed of his movements without alerting the trolls to his presence. As the Dr moved to the doorway he could clearly see inside the room. It was lit with large candles and cluttered with the skulls of many creatures which had come here to meet their demise. He also saw a young beautiful woman tied to a chair with ropes, she had dark brown hair and wore black robes and high heeled shoes; she dressed like a witch but certainly didn't look like one. Alongside the young woman in the room were two enormous trolls, each of them standing at around twelve feet tall, dwarfing the ordinarily sized female beneath them. The two trolls had short black hair which covered their large heads, they also had muscular bodies and sported various leather garments, such as wrist straps and what looked like a tatty leather kilt covering their lower body. The two trolls looked very similar to one another apart from one of them having a bristly beard covering its chin. Neither one of them looked clean and they did not look to be in an understanding mood. The young female cried and whimpered whilst sitting in the chair, the trolls yelled at her demanding she do as they ask.

"Use your magic for what we ask witch and you will be returned home!" groaned one of the trolls. The female didn't answer and continued to cry.

"She's not listening to you Trodge" said the other troll in a concerned and seemingly baffled tone of voice.

"Don't you think I know that Tarcus you blithering idiot!" replied the other troll sounding wiser and more authoritative. It was unclear what the troll's intentions were but they seemed to be getting agitated. Dr Stantham backed away from the doorway and went back to the others, he took off the Tarnhelm and walked to Alaya.

"There are two trolls in there, Trodge and Tarcus I believe their names are, there is also a young and quite beautiful woman, but I don't know if it is Aldrien because I have never seen her" said Dr Stantham informatively.

"I have seen her before, give me the Tarnhelm I will take a look" said Alaya as she wanted to be sure they were about to rescue the right person. She disappeared and went to the doorway to look into the room. Soon she re-joined with the others and confirmed that it was Aldrien the trolls held captive.

"I thought you said Aldrien was a witch?" Gordon asked Alaya,

"She is, why do you ask that?" replied Alaya,

The Distant Glimmer

"Dr Stantham said she is beautiful!"

"That doesn't mean she isn't a witch, not all of them have wrinkly faces, long noses and warts you know Gordon!" replied Alaya with a little annoyance.

"How are we going to get her out of there without either her or one of us being killed by the trolls?" said a worried Professor Cumbridge,

"I have a plan, though you may not like it" said Alaya, "I think one of us should wear the Tarnhelm and sneak into that room, the rest of us will then cause a distraction and lead the trolls away from her, we then untie Aldrien from her bonds and head for the doorway before sealing the trolls in here with all of us hopefully having made our escape!" continued Alaya,

"You are sure this will work?" asked Pholus,

"We have no other choice" replied Alaya. Alaya then once again placed the Tarnhelm on her head, and vanished from sight. She made her way to the room with the trolls and Aldrien. She crept into the room with careful precision without making a sound. she entered the room and stood next near two large wooden clubs. As Alaya stood with her beating frantically in her chest, there suddenly came a flash of light and a loud bang from the hall. Dr

Stantham was standing with others holding on tightly to the wand that Rosina had given them. He had used the wand to create a distraction.

"What was that?" said Trodge has he looked towards the direction of the noise and the light.

"I don't know Trodge" replied Tarcus,

"Follow me you, and witch, don't you go anywhere, I'll be back before you know it!" Trodge snapped before heading for the door. Both of the trolls picked up one of the wooden clubs, with Alaya only inches away from being touched as they lent across her. It was too close for comfort but the trolls left the room leaving only Alaya and a sobbing and shaking Aldrien in the room. Alaya walked over to Aldrien and she removed the Tarnhelm, causing herself to reappear before Aldrien. Adrien let out a scream of shock,

"It is ok Aldrien, it is me, Alaya!"

"What are you doing here" replied Aldrien with tears still running down her face,

"It is a long story, we need to focus on getting you out of here!" said Alaya before placing the Tarnhelm on the ground and reaching over to untie the bonds which were fixing Aldrien to the chair. Aldrien stood on her feet and Alaya picked up the Tarnhelm once again.

"Come quickly, I have friends in the hallway and those trolls are now out there with them!" said Alaya before leading Aldrien out of the candle lit room and into the dark hallway. As Alaya and Aldrien began walking down the hallway, shouting could be heard coming from distance echoing down the hall.

"Alaya, come quickly, we must get out of here!" shouted the voice of Pholus. He seemed anxious and desperate for Alaya to meet with them again. Alaya and Aldrien ran down the hallway and they soon saw the trolls standing cornering the scientists and the centaurs. Trodge lifted his club into the air and struck Bienor over the head with his club. Bienor collapsed on the floor and then Trodge hit him for a second time. Alaya screamed at the sight she had witnessed, however her screams also alerted the trolls to her presence. Tarcus turned and saw the two females standing in the darkness, he headed for them with his club in hand.

"How dare you enter the caves of the troll's centaurs!" said Trodge with fury raging in his voice.

Alaya and Aldrien tried backing away. Then from the distance there came yet another light, it lassoed its way around Tarcus and pinned him to the ground, and as he fell pieces of rock and dust dropped from the ceiling. Dr Stantham used the wand to disarm Tarcus with a paralysis enchantment. Trodge expressed his anger at what he had seen and turned his fury on Dr Stantham. Pholus, Nessus and Elatus stepped forth and drew their swords from their sheaths upward toward Trodge. Alaya came from behind him and sliced the back of his left leg with a knife. The others continued moving forward, gaining on Trodge with their swords in the air. Trodge admitted defeat and picked up Tarcus before dragging him back up into the dark hallway.

"Quick let's get out of here before either he comes back or more of them attack us from the darkness!" said Pholus before leading the way down to the end of the hall,

"What about Bienor?" said Professor Lockley

"We can't do anything for him now, we must leave him!" replied Pholus. The company continued to walk and eventually they left the mountain, walking back out of the mountain side doorway. Upon making it back outside Alaya took the wand in her hand and closed the door to mountain sealing the trolls inside.

"Thank you so much, all of you, and Alaya I am sorry about Bienor, if there was anything I could have done I would have been sure to do it" said Aldrien before sitting on the ground breathing a sigh of relief.

"You are welcome Aldrien, but we wanted to save you for a reason, we are in dire need of your help" replied Alaya without hesitation. Aldrien did not know what it was that they needed but she felt indebted to them for having helped her.

"Let us go to Eldrador, I will provide you with somewhere to rest and something to eat, and of course then I will provide you with whatever help you require," said Aldrien to the remaining company. They made their way back down the mountain side and headed back toward Eldrador with Michael seeming to be lost in a gaze at the beauty of Aldrien.

13

Land of the Sorcerers

Étoile's hope was beginning to fade and he now questioned whether or not he would live to see the end of the week. He was being held captive within a dark carriage which was being pulled along by two large black horses which bellowed smoke from their nostrils. Akaz and his red soldiers circled overhead on ghost horses and darkly clad black eyed beings rode nearby. The old black carriage also contained Malvo. He sat opposite a chained and dishevelled Étoile looking at him with his old dark eyes. Étoile tried to refrain from making eye contact with the old man as when he did he felt as though his soul was burning inside his body. The carriage had two small windows either side that allowed Étoile to look out and see the journey he was being taken on. As the carriage made progression along its course to an unknown destination, he saw and could feel rocky roads, he also saw trees and shrubs all around them as well as

THE DISTANT GLIMMER

many distant mountain ranges which stood in eyes view. As Étoile tried to take his mind of the creepy old man, Malvo began to speak in a hushed yet formidable tone.

"I suppose now is a good time to tell you where you are going human,"

"Yes I suppose it would creep!" snapped Étoile trying his best to hide the fear which resided within him,

"No need to get nasty human, I would lighten my mood if I were you, especially as these next days will be your last," said Malvo. Étoile felt his heart beating faster in his chest and his fear grew ever stronger with each passing second.

"I still don't understand what you want with me, and how did you know I was even on this planet, me and my friends had only been here one short day and you came after us attacking the centaurs. Me and the other scientists were only here to research and collect information from this planet!" said Etoile with innocence as he tried to figure out what Malvo wanted.

"You were never here to collect information, everything that has happened to you over the past few days has all been down to me, and the work of my followers" said Malvo.

"I don't understand," said Etoile

"Do you really think your commander would have sent novices with little or no field experience like yourselves into space?" Malvo said as he rhetorically questioned Étoile, "and do you really think that the mediocre technology that you humans have would have allowed you to find our advanced planet which has lay hidden from the universe for millions of years?" Malvo continued. Étoile did not know how to answer. He looked on in shock at the old man as he came to terms with what he was hearing, he also realised that the doubt his father once had, was justifiable.

"My men were following my orders all this time, your commander was under my influence, that is why he sent you on this expedition, and it was I who allowed you scientists to find this planet!" continued Malvo with a hint of enjoyment.

"I don't understand why you would do this, why do you want me?" replied Etoile.

"You can see for yourself human, I am no longer youthful and time has not been kind to me. You on the other hand are still young and energetic with lots of life ahead of you that is why you are here human… I want your life!" said Malvo harshly.

THE DISTANT GLIMMER

"But...why us? Out of everyone on planet earth why choose a group of scientists from a small research facility?" said Etoile with confusion.

"I needed someone who wasn't from this planet, someone who was young and had all of their youth still intact. We began our search of the universe and the first planet we came across was yours. We found your facility and hacked into your technology, your computers and your telescopic equipment. Hacking your systems allowed me to found out that you monitored the universe and we also found out that many young youthful men worked there, which was exactly what I need, it was perfect!" replied Malvo followed by a thin smile.

"So what happens now? Where are we going?" Etoile asked.

"We journey to Prévalo, the land of the sorcerers. It was once my home before they banished me and gave me a cursed half-life, a life as one of these black eyed beings. However the curse enabled me to become their leader because of the power I have as a sorcerer. They looked up to me, and hoped that I could also free them from their dark, lonely and cursed lives... I wont of course, this journey is purely for my benefit, but these pathetic creatures do not need to know that do they human?" said Malvo with a blood curdling tone.

"So you were once a sorcerer, what did you do to get banished?" said Etoile as he confronted Malvo. The old man did not seem to like the words that Étoile spoke and he gave him a stare that made Étoile feel uncomfortable.

" I was an outcast, they hated me because of the power I had, and that the way I could use magic was far more superior. I created a source of magic that could alter lives and make people stronger, but of course, naturally the other sorcerers were totally against me and they worked together to curse me and banish me from their land!" said Malvo as he began expressing anger.

"So why are you going back there?" asked Étoile,

"I want that source of magic back, once I have it back in my clutches I can get my power and my life back that is why I need you human… I am going to transfer all of your life, both the years you have lived and the years you could have lived into my own body and soul. I will be young, strong and powerful again and I can be the one who rids this planet of all other sorcerers… I will be the one who this planet kneels before!" Malvo continued

The Distant Glimmer

with sincerity in his harrowing tone. As Étoile heard the dark words that poured from the old man's wrinkly lips all he could do was begin to think the worst of what fate had lying in wait for him. Malvo's journey to the land of the sorcerers continued across the rocky terrain, with the ghost horses and black eyed beings flying overhead.

Unbeknownst to them, the fate of the planet and the life of Étoile now lay in the hands of Dr Stantham and the others. The help of Aldrien was all that stood between the Dr and the company getting to the land of the sorcerers and rescuing Étoile.

14

The Soothsayer

"It is not in the stars to hold our destiny but in ourselves."

"Here we are, please come through" said Aldrien as she finally allowed the company access to Eldrador through the old iron gates. As the company entered they immediately saw the dark village that lay ahead of them. There was old wooden houses which stood side by side with crooked walls and crooked roofs. Some houses had holes caused by rot allowing the light from inside to seep out. The ground beneath the company's feet was not marble or rock, it was instead large flat pieces of grey unevenly carved stone. Old trees stood with enormous trunks and their roots protruded from the cobble stones. There were also old oak trees and weeping willows adorning every available space of the dark and damp realm. The trees caused Eldrador to be constantly overshadowed by darkness, with light from above unable to pass through the dense layers of leaves and branches that formed a natural canopy overhead. The air was damp and heavy and it smelt of smoke and other unrecognizable scents. In the centre of Eldrador the company noticed a water well standing centralised in the middle of all the old houses which circled around it. Many witches were seen walking around the realm, each of them dressed in black robes. There were small witches, thin ones and plump ones, there were also old witches and young witches, some maybe as young as five years old. They were all dressed the same and none of them seemed welcoming toward the company as they walked cautiously through the village. The witch's familiars were also scattered in almost every inch of Eldrador, black cats patrolled the area with their large amber eyes staring at the new visitors, and owls of many different colours, shapes and sizes perched on trees and looked down with their large piercing eyes at the company of strangers who had entered their home. Other animals such as large toads and jet black crows also filled the surrounding areas, all of whom seemed inquisitive and came closer to the visitors.

As the company entered Eldrador they noticed a familiar face, but this time they were not looking at it from behind a gate; it was Rosina. She looked down at the floor trying to hide herself from the company and from Aldrien, but Aldrien had seen her and addressed her instantly,

"Do not try and hide yourself Rosina, I have seen you!" said Aldrien,

"Oh Aldrien it is you, I am glad to see you have returned" replied Rosina making out she hadn't noticed her.   "You have also brought the men and centaurs back with you I see" Rosina continued,

"You have met them before?" Aldrien asked Rosina,

"I have once before, they came here looking for you and I told them where to find you" Rosina replied,

"I see, and once you told them where I was they came to save my life. They saved the life of a stranger, yet someone such as yourself whom I have known all my life did not even try and contribute even the slightest effort towards trying to rescue me from those mountain trolls!" said Aldrien with annoyance in her voice,

"I am sorry Aldrien, I was…" Began Rosina, but she was immediately cut off by Aldrien,

"Don't say anymore, I don't want to hear it, I am back now, but you are for the time being no friend of mine!" continued Aldrien, "Come my friends we will go to my home, there you can rest and we can talk" said Aldrien as she made her way through the dark village turning her back on old Rosina. The company followed closely behind her and Michael and Gordon expressed looks of worriment and angst as they looked around at the many witches and dark creatures.

"Why are there so many trees around here Aldrien? It makes everywhere so dark" Michael asked,

"These trees are used for many reasons, the most important use for them is being able to use their bark and wood in order to craft our wands" replied Aldrien.

"How do you craft them?" asked Gordon inquisitively,

"In order to create a wand you must first choose a tree specific to the types of spell you will be wanting to perform, a ceremonial dagger called the Athame is then used by witches or wizards to carve out a section of the tree, such as a piece of oak or olive, this wood is then fashioned into the shape of a wand; it can be any shape the witch or wizard desires, then finally a wand fashioning spell is recited out loud,

> *'The wood I take is not mine alone,*
>
> *I do not cut for blood nor bone,*
>
> *This wood is cut for the wand to live*
>
> *Its power is thine, not mine to give,'*

The wand is then finished with crystals, stones or the emblem of that particular wizard or witch" Aldrien answered.

Aldrien eventually came to one of the old wooden houses and she stopped.

"Here we are, this is my home" she said before stepping forth and opening its door. She stepped inside followed by the others, and as they entered the house they noticed that it wasn't very big at all. It was very cluttered and had antiquities and wooden furniture covered with magical implements. There were also many shelves filled with old books with mostly unpronounceable names. There was also a fire place which hadn't been lit for a while and all that sat inside it was a cold, empty and black cauldron over some grey ashes and a pieces of wood which were the remnants of a past fire. At the far end of the room was a desk which was topped with letters and a skull which had been polished so much it reflected the items that surrounded it. The skull seemed to be acting as a paperweight for the letters which had been strewn across the surface of the barely visible desk beneath.

"I know it is not very big in here but it is only I who live here usually, it is also very cluttered I know but amazingly, I know where everything is" giggled Aldrien whilst giving a smile toward the company.

"Why did those trolls want you Aldrien?" asked Alaya,

"The trolls of Mount Malevolence are clever creatures, people often assume that mountain trolls are big and stupid, but this is not always the case. The ones that live up there knew that I was the only witch in this village with soothsaying abilities. Although their intentions for the use of my powers were not very clever. You see all they think about is food and what they will eat next, but mountain trolls cannot go out when it is light, which is why they remain in the dark mountains and then only come out at night to get their food. However, they had come to realise that searching for food in the dark was not easy, so they needed my ability to look into the future to find out where there next meal would be heading, so that they could get there first" replied Aldrien.

"I see, but wouldn't they have let you go afterwards?" Alaya continued,

"They were beating me as I would not provide them with my help, my stubbornness had the better of me and I refused to let them persuade me otherwise, they would not have let me go had I helped them. They would have just eaten me there and then" replied Aldrien, "however, you saved my life just in time and it is now my turn to return the favour as I am indebted to you all. Who is the one who requires my help?" continued Aldrien before turning and sitting down at her desk,

"That would be me" said Dr Stantham as he stepped forward in front of the company, "we are all on a quest to save the life of my son from the captivity of some dark creatures, who only days ago unleashed their full fury upon the realm of Valosia, home to these here centaurs, killing the father of my young friend Alaya" Dr Stantham continued.

"I gather you need me to help you find out where he is Dr?" asked Aldrien,

The Distant Glimmer

"Yes, this is why we had to save you from the trolls, as your help is of the utmost importance to us and we implore you to do all you can to provide us with some information regarding the whereabouts of my son" replied a desperate Dr Stantham,

"I will of course help you Dr, but I must warn you, having the ability to foresee future events must always be used sparingly, and the future that I see, may not always be the events that will come to pass, as the images I see are not always clear" warned Aldrien,

"I understand, but this is our only hope of continuing the quest, and any help you can offer will benefit us in the near future" replied Dr Stantham.

"Please take a seat next to me Dr," said Aldrien as she pointed to the old chair next to her own. As the Dr sat down Aldrien reached across her desk and pulled forth a crystal ball,

"This is my speculum, it is the implement most widely used for scrying or predicting the future, I use it as it gives me the most accurate predictions of what the future may hold" Aldrien explained before leaning forth to gaze into the large crystal ball which rested on a circular golden frame. She let her mind go blank and held a steady gaze at the crystal's light for a few moments. Before long she found herself seeing something in the crystal which caused her eyes to widen and her face to express a look of dismay. As well as seeing into the near future and witnessing how the Dr's quest would need to continue, she also gained information regarding the Dr and his son. She saw the events that had already taken place between the two of them, but apart from the Dr she also began finding out information about the darker forces which were at work. She had seen the black eyed beings, and small parts of the overlords plan. Soon she broke the gaze that she was becoming lost in and she pushed the crystal away from her causing it to roll across the desk and become trapped in between two large piles of unevenly sized old books. Aldrien looked at the Dr. then tried her best to prepare enough courage to tell him and the rest of the company what it was the speculum had forced upon her eyes.

She turned almost immediately to the Dr.,

"I am afraid Dr, the images I have seen are not the nicest, I will tell you however that if what I have seen is correct then your son is alive!" said Aldrien as she stared into Dr Stantham's eyes.

The Distant Glimmer

"Who has with him? And where are they heading? We need to know where he is being taken" replied the Dr with anger gripping every word that he spoke,

"I understand you have already seen the enemy for yourselves, those dark creatures that entered your realm and killed some of those most dear to you, they are the ones that still have your son," continued Aldrien,

"Is it the one who stole him from in front of my eyes, the man with the red coat?" asked the Dr,

"No, I am afraid he was just the dogs body, the one who acts as leader around the black eyed beings and gets given jobs to do by his master" replied Aldrien,

"Then who has my son? And what does he want with him?" anxiously asked the Dr whilst having moved forward to the edge of his seat showing he was urgently in need of more information,

"An old man by the name of Malvo has him, he is also known to many in this world, as the overlord. I knew this man many years ago, when I was a young witch first becoming familiarised with magic. I heard tales of the 'Marvellous Malvo' as he was known as one of the best wizards and sorcerers of his time. However, his fame was not set to last as he soon began work on an object of immense power. Malvo wanted to live forever so that he could keep his popularity and fame for as long as possible, the magical implement that he created was similar to a crystal ball. It was a large spherical object that gleamed and glistened with many colours that moved like a mist within it. The object gave off the most blindingly white light ever seen, almost as if it was showing the world how powerful it really was. It was beautiful to look at and it sat upon a golden dragon's hand, with its five claws reaching up its sides making it seem as if a dragon was holding it in its grasp. Malvo called it the Crystállum, and he treasured it more than anything else he had ever created or owned!" said Aldrien as she explained more about the past of the man who had taken Étoile.

"What happened to him? Why did he become the man he is today, kidnapping other people's family and terrorising villages?" asked a dumfounded Professor Lockley,

"The Crystállum is no ordinary magical implement Professor, it has the power to drain the life from other beings on this planet. Malvo could use it to take the life of another and give it to himself. The other sorcerers around him became filled with anger and hatred as it was against the ancient rules of sorcery. The leaders of Prévalo 'the land of the sorcerers, the most powerful and the oldest of them, joined forces and banished Malvo from their land and forced him to live among the social outcasts that were the black eyed beings, and they gave him a cursed half-life," replied Aldrien.

"What happened to the Crystállum" asked Professor Lockley,

"The sorcerers kept it to use it for its light, as our planet was once in total darkness every minute of the day, except for candle light. We did not have our own sun to give us natural light as your planet does. The light that the Crystállum emitted was powerful enough to light the entire planet. Every twelve hours the Crystállum is lowered out of sight, so that the planet can once again be dark, doing this gives the effect of day and night, and it allows our planet to keep track of time and have set periods where we can sleep and where we can wake for the new day," replied Aldrien.

"I still don't understand why he has my son Aldrien" asked the Dr with even more angst in his voice,

"The sorcerers placed a curse on Malvo and the Crystállum stopping him from ever using the implement of magic to take the life of someone from this planet. But the curse did not stop him from using the life of someone not from this planet" said Aldrien, as she tried her best to break the news to the Dr gently,

"So what you're saying is he wants to kill my son with this crystal ball so that he can become stronger and live longer again?" asked the Dr,

"I am afraid so Dr, I also regret to inform you that you being here on this planet was not because of an expedition, it was because of Malvo. He is the one who brought you all here, not your commander" continued Aldrien with sincerity.

"We have been used? But I don't understand!" said the Dr with confusion in his voice,

"Your commander did not know Dr, he was under their control as was any other important person around you at that time, they were not to know what was truly at work here" replied Aldrien,

" I still need to get my son back, where is Malvo taking Étoile?" asked Dr Stantham,

"He is heading for the Land of the Sorcerers, you need to get there first if you are to stop his plan from taking effect" replied Aldrien,

The Distant Glimmer

"How are we to get there before him?" asked Professor Lockley with interest,

"You will need to take a short cut across the land if you are to reach the sorcerers before them, as they will have had a day's head start on you. The short cut will involve you passing through Smugglers Cove where the two large mountain ranges meet. Once you pass through, you will need to make your way across the Sea of Sirens, only then will you be able to reach the Land of the Sorcerers and save your son!" Aldrien said with a stern seriousness in her voice.

"I know the way there, I have been passed there many times when we have been in battle and on patrol of the surrounding realms of this planet" said Pholus reassuringly.

"Thank you for all of your help Aldrien" said Dr Stantham,

"It was the least I could do Dr, after all you did save my life. If there are any resources you require please collect them before you leave us," replied Aldrien

15

Smugglers Cove

Eldrador was still dark as the company left Adrien's home. However, they noticed that the planet outside of the realm was also once again dark. The company now knew why the planet went dark so suddenly, it was because of the Crystállum.

"I am glad we met gentlemen, especially you Dr, you are a truly brave man, and I wish you and your friends luck on your journey to Smugglers Cove, it isn't too far away from here and I don't think anything will stand in your way between here and there" said Aldrien reassuringly.

"Thank you, I hope to see you again one day, I couldn't be more grateful for the help you have provided," replied Dr Stantham before raising his hand to say goodbye. Aldrien smiled and watched as the company walked further and further away, all the time nearing the iron gates. Alaya noticed Rosina still standing near the gates, but she looked unhappy, maybe because she had realised what little she and the other witches had done to save Aldrien. Alaya parted the company for a brief moment and she made her way across to Rosina.

"We are leaving now Rosina, I thought I would come and give you back your wand," said Alaya as she reached into her satchel and held up the wooden magical implement.

"Keep it child, you will be needing it more than I, there is no need for a wand in my life anymore, I am getting old, I have only one duty now and that is to stand guard at the gates of Eldrador" replied Rosina. Alaya had noticed the sadness in her eyes and she moved forward to place her hand on Rosina's shoulder to provide the frail witch with some comfort.

"I am sure Aldrien will find forgiveness in the future, you are one of her friends, she is back home now and she is safe, I am sure that she isn't the type of person to hold a grudge, speak to her, tell her how you feel, I am sure she will understand" said Alaya with a quiet and soft voice.

"Thank you Alaya, I will speak to her, in time maybe our friendship can be rekindled" replied Rosina. Alaya smiled then turned to re-join the others. Rosina stepped forwards and opened one of the large gates to allow the company to step out onto the planets rocky terrain once again. The Dr turned and smiled toward Aldrien and she smiled in return. He then walked through the gates until he was out of Adrien's sight.

***

    Etoile was still being held captive in the carriage with Malvo, his hands bound in rope behind his back constantly restricting his movements. Malvo and the black eyed beings were nearing the Land of the Sorcerers with each passing second. However, Malvo's carriage suddenly came to a halt. He peered around and tried to look out of the window but was unable to see anything. He began expressing confusion and then heard in the distance what sounded like the screams of people dying and in pain, and the sounds of horses groaning and screeching. Malvo became more curious and unsettled, before suddenly there appeared one of the black eyed beings. It swooped down from above on its fiery beast, and appeared at the window of Malvo's carriage. Étoile looked on with curiosity as he too did not know what was happening. A deep, dark and mysterious voice then came from beneath the hood of the black eyed creature. It was the first time Étoile had heard one of the creatures speak, and the sound of it made him shiver with fear.

"We are under attack my lord!" it said,

"What is it? Why are you not dealing with it you fools, what could possibly be that powerful?" snapped Malvo as he became angered,

"There are Cyclopes my lord, three of them!"

"Where is Akaz?" asked Malvo,

"He fled master, and the red soldiers went with him!"

"That coward, if I ever meet him again, his life will not be worth living!" Malvo shouted angrily, with the veins on his forehead beginning to appear more prominent, "Deal with them, NOW!" Malvo continued with his anger still visible. The black eyed being fled from the carriage and went to the aid of the others, and true to his word there stood three enormous figures. Each of them had only the one eye situated in the middle of their heads underneath an angry looking frown. They had long black unwashed hair and they wore silver armour from head to toe which had dents and scratches. The Cyclopes didn't look clean and they had streaks of dirt covering their faces. They each looked very similar and were of equal height. They towered over the many black eyed beings beneath them and they held onto swords and clubs which they used to knock the creatures from their horses, causing them to plummet through the air. Malvo's army couldn't match the pure strength and savagely fierce temperament of the three Cyclopes. The Cyclopes continued to cut the air with their swords and large wooden clubs killing all that stood in their path. Malvo and his black eyed beings had unwittingly entered their territory on their journey to the Land of the Sorcerers. The black eyed beings tried their hardest to reach the Cyclopes and strike them down, but they were no match for them. The Cyclopes moved forth across the narrow path that Malvo had come to be on. Mountain ranges surrounded them and Étoile was trapped inside the carriage with the old man, unable to break away. They were trapped and unable to move forth. The path that Malvo was on was high up in the mountains and they could not turn around without the risk of falling down the sheer drop that the mountain had formed from its cliff face. Bolts of lightning flashed and flickered through the air as the black eyed beings tried with all their might to smite the Cyclopes; but none of them had any effect on the optically impaired creatures who

The Distant Glimmer

continued to move closer to Malvo's carriage, swinging their swords and clubs in the air. Many deceased black eyed beings lay on the floor, and the flames within the eyes of the ghost horses had been extinguished.

"Why don't you do something old man, if you are as powerful as you say you are surely these creatures are no match for you?" said Étoile trying to encourage Malvo to sort the problem out for himself.

"Silence human!" snapped Malvo in reply,

"You are losing your army old man, are you sure you want to sit here and let this happen, we are going to be on the menu for those monsters" continued Étoile as he knew he was the only one powerful enough to deal with the threat that was heading their way. Outside the carriage the battle raged on and more black eyed beings tried and failed to stop the Cyclopes. Malvo eventually listened to his prisoner and climbed out from within his carriage. His frail body walked a short distance before noticing the angry rugged beasts before him. They also noticed him and made their way through the dead bodies and towards Malvo.

"How dare you infect our territory with your creature's old man, your punishment for this will be for us to enjoy having you for our next meal!" said one of the Cyclopes in a deep and menacing tone as it threatened Malvo.

The Cyclopes began running along the narrow rocky path towards Malvo swinging their weaponry over their heads in anger. However, Malvo was not fazed and he stood his ground before reaching for his staff. He thrust it into the air summoning unknown powers, and the purple mists in the night sky that once drifted in front of the stars began swirling violently, causing a tornado to form. The Cyclopes stopped their progression towards Malvo and they looked up at the storm that the old man was conjuring. Malvo seemed to be struggling but he kept up the magic and the sorcery forcing the tornado that was now pulsing with streaks of lightening and electro static energy towards the Cyclopes. The tornado picked up the dead bodies of the black eyed beings and the ghost horses, until eventually reaching the enormous monsters. It picked them up along with the other bodies like leaves caught in an updraft. Malvo sent the tornado hurling up into the dark skies with the screams now coming from the Cyclopes.

"Let us go old man, we will leave you alone!" said another of the Cyclopes now appearing scared and cowardly. Malvo did not listen to their

The Distant Glimmer

pleas and cries of terror. He continued thrusting the tornado further into the night skies before ending the spell and dropping his staff to the ground. He himself then dropped to the floor seeming to have lost even more of his energy. The tornado disappeared from above taking the three Cyclopes with it. All went quiet, and more tranquil in the after math of the events that had come to pass. Many black eyed beings had died and Akaz had fled when greeted with fear. There were hardly any of Malvo's army left, and it was a setback that he had not accounted for. Malvo stood back on his feet, and picked up his staff before heading back towards the carriage.

"Attach more horses to my carriage, I want the remainder of this journey to be airborne, I do not want any more setbacks." said Malvo as he ordered one of the black eyed beings before getting back into his carriage. He and Étoile exchanged no more words. Malvo looked worse than he ever had, and he was now even more desperate to find the Crystállum.

***

The planet was still dark and the stars still shone brightly overhead as Dr. Stantham and the others traversed the planet once again. All was quiet and even the gentlest of breezes couldn't be felt upon the skin. Soon the walking came to a halt when Pholus alerted the others of what he could see nearby.

"Over there, I can see the cove" Pholus said before pointing to where the two mountain ranges joined.

Smugglers Cove was ancient, and had been given the name many years ago as the cove had been used by dark witches and wizards who partook in evil magic to attain their potions ingredients and magical implements. All that passed through the cove was forbidden to be used on the planet. Smugglers cove had not been in use for many years and had become derelict and the home of spiders and mutant creatures. The creatures had been born from the many chemicals that had passed through the cove throughout the years. Most of the creatures were the size of birds, and they patrolled the area and looked peculiar. Some had lots of eyes, and others had lots of teeth and no eyes. The cove was formed out of two long mountain ranges that had come to merge together. The cove had been formed in a triangular shape. At the far end of the cove at the point where the two mountain ranges met, there was a dark passageway.

Smugglers Cove was dark and intimidating and Michael and Gordon were fearful of what awaited them. The ground was rocky yet dirty and the air smelled of salt like sea water, and a heavy fog shrouded the company's feet as they walked.

"There's the entrance, that should lead us to the Sea of Sirens… come, follow me!" said Pholus as he ensured the others that they were in the correct place. They continued walking, nearing the dark entrance. No light could be seen and it was unknown what it was like inside. Suddenly as they walked, out of nowhere there came a shadow, a dark, tall and menacing outline of what looked like a man. The company couldn't make out, who or what it was. Pholus raised his right hand forming a fist with his fingers, informing the others to stop, he then continued to walk on ahead almost reaching the coves passage. The shadow stepped forth out of the darkness to greet Pholus, it was a man… an elderly man, with his face wrinkled with age. He had long dark hair draping over his shoulders and a bandana pushing some of it back off his face. He was dressed in a myriad of colours and many varied garments of clothing from a velvet dark green jacket to a red waist coat. It seemed that all he wore, was all he owned.

"What do you want?" said the old man. His voice sounded breathless as if his lungs could not cope with speech. Only half of his mouth opened to allow the words to seep out which made his sentence sound slightly muffled and his voice sound untypical.

"We are a company of men and centaurs on a quest of our own business, we need to pass through this cove and reach the Sea of Sirens in order for our quest to continue" replied Pholus, in an almost commanding tone. The rest of the company re-grouped with Pholus to find out who the strange man was.

"Who are you sir?" asked Dr Stantham directing his question at the man.

"I am John Longwood… Guardian of the Smuggler's Cove!" replied the elderly gentlemen.

"We are pleased to meet your acquaintance sir, but we are in dire need of passage through this cove, we are on a quest!" began Dr Stantham,

"I know, you're on a quest, your centaur friend has already informed me of this, but it seems obvious that none of you are familiar with the customs and the legend of this cove!" interrupted an abrupt John Longwood,

"I am afraid we are not, but I am sure you will tell us" said Pholus becoming annoyed.

"Do not get discourteous with me horseman!" shouted John, " I have guarded this cove for almost fifty years, following its closure, it has been my job to only let those through the cove who are truthful and really in need of its passage," continued Mr Longwood.

"We are in need of this, and we are true, we need to pass through this cove!" said Alaya as she too now began to get agitated and annoyed at the old man.

"The only way you can enter the passage of the cove is if you present me with one of your most treasured possessions. Only then can I determine if you are being true to your word... and only then can I let you pass through to the Sea of Sirens" said the old man with a certain sternness in his voice.

"But we have nothing but our satchels and some scraps of food!" said Alaya.

"We do have something Alaya, but I fear you will not want to part with it" said the Dr before reaching for his back pack, Alaya then realised what the Dr. was about to present her with,

"No, not that, there has to be something else" said Alaya with some upset. It was the Tarnhelm, the magical piece of armour and the most treasured possession of Chiron, the one piece of treasure he had guarded with his life for many years, as did his father and his father before him.

"I am sorry Alaya, you don't have to give it to the old man, but it is the only treasured possession we have, if you will not allow it to be given away, this quest will end here" said the Dr with desperation apparent in his voice.

"It is not what I want to do Dr, but it has to be done, for your son and for our world. You may give him the Tarnhelm" said Alaya with reluctance. Dr Stantham stepped forward towards John Longwood and presented him with the gleaming golden helmet. The old man took it from the Dr and gazed into its polished reflective surface; he seemed to be using the helmet for the same reasons that Aldrien had used the crystal ball. He was retrieving information regarding the company, finding out if they were truthful and truly in need of the passage to the Sea of Sirens. When he withdrew his gaze from the helmet he looked up and smiled at the Dr and then at Alaya,

"You are truthful and this quest is an important one, and if what I have seen is correct, the quest will also affect me and my life as well as your own. I do not usually do this but I see how much this means to you, you may take the helmet back and I grant you permission to enter the passage through the cove" said John before handing the Tarnhelm back to the Dr. Alaya could not thank him enough as he had been most generous.

John Longwood stepped aside leaving the passage way open, allowing the company to enter and make their way through the darkness of the mountains. The Dr was the last to enter as he stayed back for a short while to express his gratitude towards John. Finally he entered the passage way behind the others and John Longwood disappeared into the shadows to be amongst the strange and dark creatures.

Inside the passageway it was cold and narrow and extremely dark. The ground beneath their feet was soggy, almost like quick sand and felt damp because of the sea that lay ahead. The company had to feel around at first to make sure they were not stepping on something or straying from their path. However, they weren't in darkness for long as Alaya had remembered the wand that she still had in her satchel. She reached into the satchel and felt around trying to identify it with her fingertips. She eventually found its long wooden shape and withdrew it. She held it above her head, and began to think of light pouring from the wand to light up the dark passageway. Just then the wand began to oblige to her thoughts and an extremely bright light began streaming from the tip. The light was blindingly bright but it allowed the company to see far ahead of them into the passageway. They saw that it was narrow and at their sides and above their heads were many rocks which were part of the mountains they were now inside. The ground was also exactly as they thought it would be; a wet, sludgy thick consistency lay beneath their feet. A concoction of water and dirt had created something that almost glued them to the ground. It was unclear how much of the dark passage was left to walk. The company longed for the appearance of even the smallest amount of light to seep in through the exit of the passage, to indicate the first glimpses of the sea of sirens.

16

The Sea of Sirens

Soon light began to pour in through an opening at the very end of the passageway, and the outside world could be heard and smelt once again. The company had been in the suffocating small space for a long while and they now longed to be able to stretch their arms and release the tension which had built up in their muscles. A gentle breeze soon came fluttering into the passageway and the smell of salt and sea air was now more prominent than before.

"We're almost there, I can see light coming from ahead of us. I also see a slight glare and a flickering of blue light seeping into the passageway that could most likely be a reflection caused by the waters." explained Pholus. The walk to the end of the passageway was not a long one and the company soon found themselves standing amidst the blue glare that Pholus had spoken of. The first to step outside was Alaya. She soon called the others to join her, to see it for themselves. There it was, the Sea of Sirens in all its glory. A vast open space that looked like a bowl brimming with crystal clear light blue waters, waters that reflected the stars that twinkled and pulsated overhead. The company stood upon on a rocky bank that looked like a stone beach on the shoreline of the nearby sea. The surrounding area embraced nature, and more of the oddly coloured trees swayed in the breeze. The shore of the siren sea was a truly beautiful scene, and the company were tempted to lay down and forget their troubles.

    Across the Sea of Sirens, a second rocky bank could be seen before another range of mountains. The other side of the sea looked very similar to the one the company were on, however, as they surveyed the area, the Land of the Sorcerers was yet to be seen, and the only obvious way of reaching the adjacent shoreline, was to cross the open expanse of the wide open sea.

    "Forgive my ignorance but, why is it called the Sea of Sirens?" asked Michael seeming confused by the choice of name.

    "A siren is very much a creature of beauty, you may know more of what they look like if I were to call them a mermaid. They are like centaurs as they are born of two species. Where we are half man half horse, the siren, or the mermaid, is half woman half fish, hence the reason why they live in water. They enchant those who cross their waters with song, it is very easy to become left adrift with the sounds of angels creeping into your ears. Whilst you gaze into the deep blue eyes of an aesthetically pleasing female form, you become lost in a trance at their beauty, and they catch you off guard before pulling you down beneath the surface of the water, and it isn't until you pass into the depths that you realise this isn't a creature of beauty at all, but rather a creature of darkness and pure detrimental evil!" replied Pholus as he recounted what he knew of the sirens.

"I can't do this anymore!" said Professor Cumbridge having become pale in skin tone and looking as if he had suddenly become ill. He stumbled into a seated position on the rocky ground near the calm sea,

"You can't do what anymore?" replied Dr Stantham seeming confused at the professor's words,

"This, a quest into an unknown land risking our lives, we should not be doing this Bernard!"

continued Professor Cumbridge whilst looking down at his feet.

"Of course we shouldn't be here, do you really think it was my intention to have my son kidnapped then set out on a journey to save his life!" snapped an upset and angered Dr Stantham.

"We shouldn't even be on this planet Bernard, we are not trained for this, we have never left that science base since we started work there, let alone leaving earth!" said Professor Cumbridge harshly,

"We have been through this many times, we all know now that each of us were not in our right minds when we came on this expedition, yet I read the letter that our commander sent, and I couldn't believe it, when did anything exciting ever happen to us, when would we ever get a chance to journey to another planet such as this? We had discovered a new planet... or so we thought, and we were entrusted with an expedition of the utmost importance for our country, it was a once in a life time opportunity!" replied Dr Stantham with some emotion.

"You didn't really put up much of a fight though did you professor" said Professor Lockley as he tried to back up Dr Stantham, "you yourself came willingly on this mission without giving it a second thought!" Professor Lockley continued, Professor Cumbridge still looked at the floor rejecting any eye contact with the others.

"I know, but I thought it would be a derelict wide open space with no other life apart from us. I thought we would land in our craft, look around, note down some information and then go home again. I never once thought I would come face to face with creatures I had only ever read about in books… it is all a little too much for me!" replied Professor Cumbridge before burying his head in hands to hide his feelings of upset and fear.

"Chiron opened my eyes to what was really going on here Professor Cumbridge, and only then did I realise that this may have been a mistake. But, we were never supposed to get back home, this was a suicide mission created by the evil forces of this planet. We would never have been sent here under normal circumstances. I realise that now, but our commander was being commanded, he still doesn't know that we are here to this day. However, all this still doesn't alter the fact that my son has been kidnapped and all the regret in the world won't get Étoile back, only the success of this quest will do that!" said Dr Stantham with a continuing level of anger and distress in his voice.

Professor Cumbridge peered up over his arms and looked at once at Dr Stantham. He seemed to begin understanding how the Dr felt,

"You have a choice my friend, you either stay here alone under the darkness of the mountains or you come with us and finish this quest and save the life of Étoile, and all the friends we have made on this wonderful planet" Dr Stantham continued.

"I will finish this quest with you Dr, but once it is over I want to find a way of getting of this rock and going home, you may be comfortable here as you have no family back on earth, but I am far from feeling at home right now!" replied Professor Cumbridge.

"Well… that settles it then, back to the task at hand gentlemen, the more time we waste here the less time we have to get to the Crystállum before Malvo!" said Pholus. "We still need to find a way across these waters and reach the opposing bank!" continued Pholus.

"Alaya, that wand you used for the light in the passage way, couldn't you use that to conjure up some sort of a flotation device to allow us to cross the waters, such as boat or a raft" asked Elatus with sincerity. Alaya agreed it was a good idea. She also knew it was their best option. Without some protection across the sea, they would be forced to wade across with the impending deaths at the hands of the sirens looming over them.

    Alaya once again reached inside her satchel and retrieved the wand. She held the wand up before her and tried her best to imagine something on the water that would allow her and the company to cross the Sea of Sirens with ease. Soon the wand caused reality to force itself into action as the water closest to them began to ripple in circles, spreading out further and further out to sea. The ripples began to expand and grow ever bigger signalling that something big was about to greet them on the water's surface.

    "What are you thinking about Alaya? Are you sure we need something this big?" said Elatus as he backed away from the water's edge as he was unsure what would be rising from the depths. Alaya continued focusing on her thoughts with her eyes closed tightly allowing the images within her mind to become ever more vivid. The water continued to move. Then before the eyes of the company came the appearance of what looked like the bow of an enormous ship piercing the clear water's surface. The sound of the water crashing on the sides of the ship became deafeningly loud. As the ship began to surface it was noticeable almost instantaneously that it wasn't wet. It was arriving from the depths of the sea but was completely dry. The eyes of the scientists became filled with joy for a brief moment, and the quest they were on was forgotten for those few moments as the ship revealed itself in all its glory.

Soon the ship was finally fully visible, floating upon the water's surface, with a majestic magnificence.

"Is it real?" asked Michael still struggling to believe what his eyes were seeing,

"So much for a little boat or raft then Alaya!" said Elatus with a smile; Alaya smiled back, with a hint of surprise at what she had created.

The ship was dark brown and stood as high as three single decked buses. It had sails which bore the emblem of Valosia with the centaurs standing opposite each other with their swords thrust into the air, like the one on the armour of the company. The sails blew wildly in the wind causing them to spread wide showing the emblem in all its glory. The ship had windows at the rear with their edges framed in bright gold, and at the bow of the ship there stood a perfectly crafted golden statue of Chiron, thrusting a sword up into the cold and crisp night air.

The Distant Glimmer

"Why did you create a ship like this Alaya?" asked the Dr,

"I thought it was the most appropriate form of transport considering we are at the smugglers cove. The size of this ship might also ward off sirens who's paths we may cross." replied Alaya as she looked at the awe inspiring and beautifully crafted ship before her.

The company took it in turns to climb aboard, even Professor Cumbridge, who had seemed to once again gather some courage to continue the quest even though everyone knew he did not want to be part of it.

The ship had been docked near the rocky bank in such a way that allowed the company to easily gain access to the deck of the ship. A wooden stairway sloped downward from the ship above and greeted the company at their feet allowing them to walk up and find a place on the polished wooden surface of the deck. When everyone boarded Pholus pulled the stairway up with some rope allowing the side of the ship to become complete.

Not one of the scientists nor the centaurs knew how to control a ship of such size, but they were in luck as the ship began to move off of its own accord. There was no wheel at the helm of the ship showing that it could not be manually steered; it was almost as though the ship knew where the company were heading.

The company began to enjoy the comforting motion that the ship made as it gently parted the water's surface. The sound of the water was also calming as it rushed down the sides of the ship; a trickling noise could softly be heard as the water was pushed away by the stern. However the relaxing journey was not what the Sea of Sirens had planned for the company. The water began to ripple around the ship, and the ripples were too far out to have been caused by the motion of the ship itself. The company had a notion of what may have been causing the ripples. It was the first signs that the sirens were nearby, and closing in on the company.

"Everyone come in close… stand in the centre of the ship, it is too dangerous to be on the sides… I do not know what stratagems these creatures could perform!" said Pholus as he tried to use his wisdom and knowledge of the Sirens to protect the others.

"Have you been in contact with these creatures before Pholus?" asked Gordon hoping that the answer would be yes; however disappointment soon overcame Gordon when Pholus replied "NO!"

"NO! what do you mean NO? I thought you had been here in battle many years ago with Chiron!" replied Professor Cumbridge now seeming to have once again found negativity in his thoughts,

"I never said I had meetings with the Sirens, I know of them, and yes I have been around here during battle, but I never came through that passage and I have never had to cross this sea before, I merely passed near the smugglers cove, I never actually entered!" replied Pholus,

"Do not worry yourselves we are still expert swordsmen, we should be able to hold them off if they become a threat, remember that we are soldiers and we have seen battle, so I am sure some half fish ladies cannot be that much of a danger to us!" said Elatus trying to give some words of encouragement to the more nervous of the company. However, following close behind Elatus's words of comfort came the most angelic sound they had ever heard. The song of the Sirens begun filling the air, and all other audible sounds soon became drowned out by the perfectly pitched voices which had made their way into the ear canals of the scientists and the centaurs. All but Alaya seemed to have become calmed by the sounds, so she shouted to warn them of the trap. Nessus however, one of the quieter centaurs, couldn't seem to hold off the comfort and relaxation he felt as he listened to the Sirens song. He began edging closer to the side of the ship before peering out over the edge. There they were, the Sirens, swimming around on the surface of the sea surrounding the bottom of the ship. They could only be seen from the waist up and they were the truly beautiful women that Pholus had once described. They each had long hair, of different colours, some had brown, some had blonde, some even had bright red, but it all looked like silk cascading down over their shoulders. Each of the Sirens looked and sounded like angels, bright blue eyes looked up at Nessus piercing his mind causing him to drift further into their song and become lost in their allure. Nessus lent further over the side of the ship but Pholus soon noticed his friend becoming slave to the powers of the Sirens and he immediately ran to his aid to pull him away from the side. Nessus fought him off as he had gazed at the creatures for too long and had become a mere shadow of his former self. His clear sighted mind had become hazed by the encapsulating song of the creatures from the depths below,

"Nessus, snap out of this, it's a trap, this is what they want!" shouted Pholus trying his best to save his friend. He pulled Nessus back from the ships edge causing the two of them to fall to the floor. Pholus's actions angered the Sirens as the one they had entranced hoping to feast on had been taken from them by an interfering friend. The song stopped and it turned to deafening screams. Professor Cumbridge tried to cover his ears to block out the noise as he was now even more petrified of what lay ahead. Pholus and Elatus drew their swords from their sheaths in preparation for an attack on the ship. Pholus told the scientists and Alaya to hide out of view, but none of them did. They each stood side by side; even Michael and Gordon had weapons which they taken from the weapon room within the home of Chiron. Nessus lay on the floor lost in a trance and unable regain his rational mind. The screams from the water continued and Pholus found the slightest morsel of bravery within his soul and he stepped forth to look into the waters below. He saw evil looking monsters with snarling teeth and wide red glowing eyes in place of the once angelic creatures which had lurked there only moments ago. Pholus stepped back to re-join the others. The company formed a circle to cover all angles of the ship; the only one who didn't participate in protecting each other's lives was Professor Cumbridge. He had hidden himself away in the captain's cabin.

The other all held their form, keeping their swords and knives raised in the air, with the steel of the blades catching the light of the stars; blue light shimmered down the blades with a gleam of grace.

The screams of the Sirens continued to send shivers down the spines of all who heard them. Suddenly the screams became louder and sounded closer than ever before. Pholus looked up to the stars, and saw one of the creatures launching itself through the air above their heads. It was not trying to attack the company, however, it seemed to have been pinpointing there locations on the ship, in order to be the most advantageous when executing their attack. For the first time the siren could be seen completely, it had the torso of a perfectly formed woman, but the creature had no legs, it instead looked like an gargantuan fish, with green and blue glossy scales glistening with hypnotic charm, beneath the light of the stars. The evil creature continued to fly through the air whilst maintaining eye contact with Pholus. The company tried their best to thrust their weapons up to incapacitate the creature hoping to strike it a death blow with their blades, but they could not reach it; the creature had jumped with so much force that it was at least ten feet above their heads. The Siren soon passed and the splash could be heard below as it made re-entry into the sea.

"That's not the last of them, I know it… prepare yourselves… protect Nessus!" said Pholus as he warned the others that the presence of the Sirens was still with them. Pholus was proven correct only mere moments later as more soon came. They leapt across the ship, screaming, snarling and staring at the company in the most threatening, and sadistic manner. Pholus and Elatus continued stabbing into the air hoping to bring down one of the creatures with their swords, but they continued with a lack of success. The Sirens threatened the company and began to draw in lower and closer to the scientists and centaurs, trying to grab them or cut them as they passed. Michael and Gordon didn't know whether to fight, or panic, but somehow, within them they found enough bravery to hold their ground.

Two Sirens suddenly came leaping over the ship together making a leap for Nessus who still lay on the ship's deck, in a daze unknowing what was happening around him. Pholus and Elatus tried their best to ward them off but they couldn't reach them in time. The Sirens caught hold of Nessus and plunged back into the sea with Nessus in their grasp. Pholus ran to the side of the ship in one last desperate attempt to save his friends life, but he could do no more. Nessus was gone, and the water was still.

All went quiet and the ship was filled with sadness, as yet another of Alaya's closest friends had been lost during the quest. However, she had run her tears dry and could not cry any more. Professor Cumbridge came sneaking out of the captain's cabin once again, but no one spoke to him nor greeted him as they had become tired of his ignorance and lack of help towards the others. There was also no time to grieve for Nessus. They needed to get off the ship and out the Sea of Sirens as soon as possible before the dark creatures returned to claim another life. Alaya plucked the wand out of the satchel and made the ship increase its speed.

"We should get to the other bank soon enough, I cannot stay on this sea of death much longer!" Alaya said before moving away from the others to be alone with her thoughts.

The Distant Glimmer

    The company sat in silence for the remainder of the journey to remember those who had fallen. Time continued to pass and the light of the planet was soon rekindled once again; however this time, it seemed closer, and brighter than it had been before. The sea gleamed and reflected the light from above like the oceans reflected the light of the sun back on earth, and soon the ship soon came to a stop and made birth near the rocky bank at the foot of the mountains that the company had once looked upon from afar.

    "Here we are… we must go now, there may still be time enough for us to get to the sorcerers!" said Pholus informing the others that they needed to make haste.

Each of them disembarked the ship and headed toward another passage in the side of the mountains before them, in search or Prévalo, the land of the sorcerers.

II

A Returning Foe

***

"Why don't you quit whilst your ahead old man!" snapped Étoile trying to persuade Malvo to back down.

"Silence human, haven't I warned you before of your insolence!" said Malvo in retaliation, with his ever deteriorating voice. Malvo and the black eyed creatures along with Étoile were all now airborne; they had been ever since their brush with the Cyclopes. Malvo needed to reach the Land of the Sorcerers in due time if he was going to succeed in taking hold of the Crystállum. The old maniacal dark wizard was closing in on the Land of the Sorcerers with fast progression, and with a clear objective in his mind.

The Distant Glimmer

***

Meanwhile the company were making haste, and were departing from the cover of the mountains passage. As they made their way out of the dark passageway they were greeted by a dense forestry of trees that stood tall side by side. The trees were overgrown and glistened with a majestic elegance, and the ground was littered with branches and shredded bark. Some of the trees were silver and there branches glittered from the light that peered in through the natural canopy of the forest. The circumjacent area was peaceful and birds sang songs as they fluttered their wings in the high canopies.

"Where are the rocks, I thought the planet could only be altered within the realms of those who live on the planet?" asked Dr Stantham seeming confused as to why the forest did not have the familiar rocky ground.

"This must be part of the land" replied Pholus,

"The 'land', what do you mean?" asked Professor Lockley with apparent confusion,

"I don't think we will have to go far to find the Land of the Sorcerers gentlemen, we are already in it!" replied Pholus with a tone of content.

"Come, let us walk further into this land, we may soon see someone who we can speak to" continued Pholus before leading the way through the trees and the many branches and leaves which stood in their path. It didn't seem to look like the way into the land was used very often as the trees and the ground were untouched. Pholus walked with his sword thrust into the air felling and pruning tree branches and brambles as he progressed, clearing a pathway for the others to follow.

"I don't understand though, how is it we have come to be in the Land of the Sorcerers so easily? No guards or anyone to stop us from getting in like Rosina for Eldrador!" said Professor Lockley with puzzlement.

"I feel that this passageway is some sort of secret entrance into this land, it obviously isn't used all that often, most likely because others are not witless enough to cross the Sea of Sirens!" replied Pholus with his observatory theory.

The company walked through the forest with careful precision, and before long they spotted a building. It had been constructed with old grey stones and it towered higher than anything else the company had seen. The building was crooked in shape yet looked somewhat supreme as it stood amidst a canvas of star sprinkled skies and a serene vast open land. The Land of the Sorcerers truly looked to be an enormous civilisation; and an old one too. The realm was four times the size of Valosia and six times the size of Eldrador. Many sorcerers walked slowly and calmly throughout the land as the company stood at the edge of the forest taking in the awe inspiring sights before them. There were male sorcerers and female sorcerers patrolling the realm of Prévalo, and they walked casually and slowly, and seemed to be a peaceful people.

Beyond the large tower their bustled a village of old wooden homes and small lakes and ponds with wooden bridges all noticeably hand carved. The entirety of the realm was also surrounded by high peaked mountain ranges and the scientists also noticed that there was grass surrounding the lakes; it was the first time they had seen grass since their arrival on the planet. The grass was bright green in colour and had been trimmed to perfection. Rolling hills framed the scene, flowing from the grassy patches with their reflections being caught in the calm waters of the rivers, lakes and small ponds that had found a natural home under trees. The sounds of gentle water flowing down through rivers and crashing into rocks also caressed the ears and brought calmness to the mind. The air smelled fresh and the floor was the same as the forest floor, flat and level but merely formed from dirt.

"We can't stand in this forest forever we need to find someone who we can speak with, they need to be warned of the impending threat, I am sure Malvo isn't too far away from here now!" said Pholus as he prompted the others to follow him out of the forest.

The company managed to walk only a few paces from the edge of the forest when they were spotted by an old man who had been standing by a gate. It looked as though the old man had the same role as Rosina in Eldrador, a gatekeeper. The man had a long pearly white beard and equally long white hair to match. His hair waved around and lapped at his face as he marched toward the company with an angry expression upon his face, and a frown set deep into his forehead, which highlighted his many wrinkles. The old man wore old brown boots and a purple robe which dragged along the floor. His robe had large sleeves which also flapped around in the wind, and around the old man's waist was a large belt with a red gemstone used for a buckle. He continued walking towards the company making his way in the direction of Pholus, and suddenly he began to shout. At first it was inaudible, but eventually the air carried the slight sound of what he was saying,

"Who are you? How did you get in here? You are not allowed in here without my permission, and I most certainly didn't grant it to you!"

"We are sorry sir, we came through the forest, we thought it strange that we came in so easily, we mean you no harm" replied Pholus as he tried to befriend the man.

"You mean us harm! I knew it… INTRUDERS, guards come quick we have INTRUDERS!" shouted the old man in return. It became apparent that the old man was a little hard of hearing as he misinterpreted what Pholus had said. Suddenly a dozen tall muscular, well-formed men clad in armour stormed their way fiercely towards the company.

"Please gentlemen, we mean you no harm, please listen to me… it seems there has been a mistake!" said Pholus trying his best to reason with the small troop of soldiers which were now marching quite intimidatingly. Soon they reached the company and began tying lengths of rope around the centaurs and the scientist's arms, binding their hands behind their backs. The old man greeted them not too long after and stood awkwardly alongside his soldiers.

"Take them to the cabin!" said the old man with a gruff gravelly voice which seeped through his wrinkly prune like lips. The soldiers grasped one of the company members each by the ropes which bound their arms, before marching them one by one towards a wooden, cobweb ridden, termite infected cabin.

"In here!" groaned one of the soldiers who clutched tightly onto the arm of Pholus. The soldier pushed the creaky wooden door inward before forcing Pholus inside. The cabin was small and smelled damp. There wasn't much inside apart from a wooden desk and a small chair. On top of the desk there stood a metal mug filled with a black liquid of some sort which bellowed steam upward from its surface.   A few moments passed and the remaining members of the company were forcibly manhandled into the cabin to join Pholus. The old man entered the room and sat down on the small chair before looking at the company still with a frown and angry look across his face. "Guards, wait outside!" said the old man with a high level of authority.

The Distant Glimmer

"Sir, we mean you no harm here, we merely made an error in the choice of entrance we used to gain access to your land," said Alaya trying to reason with the old man. The bonds cut at her wrists as she tried her best to wriggle free, but she tried to no avail.

"How did you gain access?" said the old man he sat in his chair looking up at the company with a growing level of curiosity.

"We came through a passageway that led us into a forest behind this cabin." replied Alaya,

"No one uses that anymore, I didn't think anyone even knew it existed!"

"We have journeyed here on a quest to your land, someone we met on our journey told us of this passage, we passed through the Smugglers Cove and across the Sea of Sirens to get here" continued Alaya trying to show the truth in words.

"A quest, what sort of quest?" asked the old man,

"What is your name sir? Can we at least know who it is we are addressing?" Pholus interrupted,

"My name is Rithpin, the gatekeeper of Prévalo. My job is to keep intruders such as yourselves out of this land!" said Rithpin, "Now…

I will ask again, what is this quest you are on and why does it concern the sorcerers?" asked Rithpin, the question was open to anyone who felt they could answer, and it was again Pholus, who felt the need to speak.

"A few days ago our village"

"What village? Whose village?" interrupted Rithpin before Pholus could finish,

"Valosia, the home of the centaurs… do you know of it?" asked Pholus continuing,

"Yes of course"

"A few days ago, Valosia was attacked and ambushed, by another race of creatures that live not too far from us in in the shadowed land…do you know of this place?" asked Pholus,

"Yes I most certainly do!" Rithpin replied before signalling for Pholus to continue,

"The black eyed creatures came from Murdreddia led by a group of men dressed in red attire. They attacked our village and killed many of our people including the great Chiron, our leader and the father of Alaya," said Pholus as he pointed Alaya out to Rithpin,

"I see, but I still don't understand why that brings you here" Rithpin replied,

THE DISTANT GLIMMER

"We have been led to believe that a man by the name of Malvo, a self-appointed leader of the black eyed creatures is the mastermind behind the attack. He was not in the battle himself, but we were told that he is the one most likely to be behind all of this. During the battle a young man called Étoile, the son of my friend Dr Stantham here, was kidnapped by the black eyed beings," continued Pholus before once again being interrupted,

"How do you know of all this, who is the one that gave you such information?" asked Rithpin,

"We visited Eldrador and sought the help of Aldrien, the soothsayer, she saw images of the future and of the past and she gave us as much information as she could give about our quest," replied Pholus. However, before Rithpin could ask any more questions, another old man gracefully entered the cabin. He was taller than Rithpin and had a grey beard instead of a white one, he also wore what looked like a golden crown upon his head, and his robes were made from fine materials which had been entwined with golden leaves and silver lines of cotton. The robes reached the floor and caressed a pair of silver slippers which appeared expensive and expertly crafted. The old man looked noble and of a high rank. As he entered the room Rithpin launched himself off his seat and threw himself onto his knees beneath the sorcerers feet,

"Get up Rithpin, what is going on here?" asked the old man in a quiet yet calm voice. He didn't seem annoyed at the fact he had intruders and he came across as a very polite and understanding gentleman.

"Sorry your grace, these people were found lurking near the woods, they have been speaking of some sort of quest, and they mentioned Aldrien and…" said Rithpin before hesitating on the second name he wanted to say,

"And, who?" asked the old man

"Malvo your grace!" replied Rithpin with a short and concise answer.

"Malvo? We haven't heard that name for many years!" said the old man before turning to the company with a look of puzzlement and concern. "Can you explain yourselves?" he continued directing his question at the company,

"Of course sir, I am Pholus, we are not intruders in your land; at least not purposely… we are on a quest and we need to warn you of a threat that you and this world are about to face!" said

Pholus with a level of urgency and desperation in his tone.

"I am Zanril Warlance, one of three leaders within the high council of the Land of the Sorcerers. If there is anyone you must tell your story to, it would be me. Please walk with me. Rithpin, release them from their bonds, you have no authority to do this without first consulting me!" said Zanril with annoyance.

"Of course your grace… GUARDS!… untie our guests!" replied Rithpin now more amiable than before. The guards came back into the cabin with swords in hand and cut through the ropes.

"Come, follow me!" said Zanril once again before leaving the cabin. The company followed him outside leaving Rithpin behind. They made their way out across the dirt covered ground and towards the enormous building which they had once seen from the forest. The company saw that the top of the building was emitting the brightest light they had ever seen. It caused their minds to wonder, and they immediately thought of the Crystállum. It was Zanril's building that homed the powerful crystal, and it was there that the source of the planets light was being kept.

The company continued to walk and eventually they came to the foot of the stone steps which led up to the large wooden doorway of the regal building. Zanril led the way up the stairs and entered the building first. The company reluctantly followed him and made their way up the many steps. As they reached the top Pholus pushed open the door and entered the building. They went inside and saw Zanril walking up a winding staircase that had been constructed around the circumference of the building, climbing steeply up the walls. There were no ceilings visible from the lobby and the roof could be seen. The building was circular in shape and it looked old and untypical. Light from candles and from windows caressed every inch of the grey carved stones, and antiquities and a large coal fire in the lobby gave the building a stately feel. There were also paintings hanging from nails on every wall, with most of them being old portraits of sorcerers, most likely past members of the high council, and ancestors of Zanril.

"Please follow me, this way!" said Zanril as he continued making progression up the stone winding stairs which were leading him up to a terrifying height.. The first to begin the ascent around the buildings circular walls was Pholus. As he took his first awkward steps onto the cold stone he encouraged the others to follow him. Zanril eventually halted his ascent of the stairs next to a small and narrow black wooden doorway; the company soon joined Zanril near the door.

"Follow me, in here please," said Zanril before opening the small doorway and stepping inside. The room which the company entered was very unexpected. The room was decorated much like Zanril clothing garments. It had many expensive materials laden across the furnishings, which were also adorned with precious gems. There were also rings and other jewels which Zanril owned hanging from hooks and contained within wooden boxes atop old plinths which had been carved with inscriptions and emblems from centuries past. There was also lots of silver and gold decorating the walls and a real fur rug lay stretched out on the floor surrounded by aged red leather armchairs. The room was clean and tidy and fit for a king.

As the company entered they saw two other men very similar to Zanril sitting on the leather chairs in front of a large coal fire. They also wore crowns, but theirs were smaller than Zanril's and had been fashioned from silver and not gold. The two men also had grey beards and were fairly old, they both looked at the new arrivals with inquisitive eyes as they entered.

"I would like you to meet the two other leaders of this land, their names are Norkas and Runil" said Zanril as he proceeded with the formalities. Zanril then found himself a seat before offering the others a seat for themselves.

"Now tell me, what is this quest that you told Rithpin of?" Zanril asked Pholus,

"The black eyed creatures of the shadowed land attacked Valosia, the home of the centaurs, and they engaged us in battle and destroyed our village, killing or wounding many of our people including our leader. They then left taking with them the son of Dr Stantham who we have with us now. We came on a quest to rescue his son and to reclaim our honour. We visited Aldrien in Eldrador and she gave us knowledge which she discovered in her visions, she told us that Malvo was behind it all, and that he intends to come here." said Pholus with emotion.

"Slow down my friend, I can see you are all tired and this quest is important to you, but the name you mentioned, Malvo… it has not been heard around these parts for many years, he was once a dark wizard whom was once banished from these lands due to his meddling in the dark areas of sorcery. We cursed him and he was forced to live among the shadowed creatures." said Zanril as he told the company of what he knew of Malvo,

"We know of the Crystállum, Aldrien said that it was Malvo that created it at the height of his powers in order to try and sustain his power and his fame" replied Pholus,

"Then I am sure she also told you that we were the very men who also placed a spell upon that magical implement following the banishment of Malvo from this land. We kept the Crystállum for its light and nothing else, our planet was once in darkness, we thought we could use that crystal to provide us with light, so we placed a curse on it that would prevent Malvo and anyone else on this planet from using the Crystállum for any other purpose, including the sustaining and prolonging of life. No one on this planet can use it, so I am afraid to say it but there is nothing Malvo can do with that now!" said Zanril as he told the company of what he thought to be true,

"You say that it cannot be used by anyone from this planet, this much is true… but Malvo has been working on a plan. You see, the young man which his men kidnapped, the son of my friend here… is not from this planet" replied Pholus. A look of shock rushed to the faces of the three elderly sorcerers.

"What do you mean not from this planet?" Zanril asked,

"Malvo sent red soldiers to the planet earth to retrieve a young man, a scientist, someone who studied the universe and someone, who if taken from their own planet, wouldn't be missed or have their actions seem suspicious. The red soldiers were under Malvo's influence, they used magic on the commander of their scientific research facility, which allowed these here scientists to visit our planet for Malvo to take pickings from" said Pholus as he put the sections of the story together like a jigsaw. Zanril couldn't believe what he heard and seemed shocked that Malvo could have come up with such a plan.

"The planet earth… our sister planet… of course, how could we have been so stupid, it was only a matter of time before he came up with something like this!" said Zanril with a heavy heart.

"Sorry… what do you mean your sister planet?" asked Dr Stantham,

"Many years ago when the planet earth was forming from rocks amidst the stars of the universe, one of those rocks broke away and drifted alone among the darkness. The rock began forming a planet of its own in that darkness. It formed amidst the stars but had no moons nor suns. However, the planet was almost identical to its sister, the planet earth. It formed oceans which generated a plentiful supply of water. It also formed land which had precious stones on its surface, and it also birthed mountains and grew trees and grass, and a breathable atmosphere with oxygen, which would soon allow life to begin thriving." Zanril continued with his voice carrying the mesmerizing story toward the scientists.

"How is it you know all of this about us but we have only just come to find out about your planet. We practically live next door to each other but we never once discovered this place throughout centuries of astronomical research." asked Dr Stantham as he became more curious.

"The sorcerers during the days of old, placed a spell on our planet which allowed us to be hidden from the universe, to hide us from any threats from outsiders, the sorcerers made our planet invisible. I don't know how he did it but Malvo must have been the one who has taken away the spell. He has allowed our planet to once again be seen, and its most likely that he did it purposely as part of his plan!" replied Zanril. "It seems Malvo has once again found new ways of using his dark mind and dark magic against us, and if what you are saying is the truth, then we are once again at risk and the dark wizard is returning home" Zanril continued sounding troubled. He looked out of the window at the far side of the room, almost sensing the malevolent presence of Malvo closing in on them.

18

The Light and the Dark, The Good and the Evil

*"It is during our darkest moments that,
We must focus on seeing the light."*

"We are nearly there human, there's not long left, in every sense of the word regarding your current predicament" said Malvo menacingly. Malvo and his army were nearing the Land of the Sorcerers and it seemed that the lead that the company once had was not a very substantial one. The demon winged horses carried Malvo through the clouds and purple mists of the orange sky with the light of the Crystállum calling on them as they inched forth with every beat of their large black wings. Not many words were exchanged between Étoile and Malvo; the last words heard by Malvo on the journey were the ones he spoke as he urged the black eyed creatures to hasten their pace.

The Orbis Chronicles

***

Zanril paced back and forth in his living quarters returning his glance towards the window three times as he tried his best to figure out how he was going to hold off the impending threat.

"Norkas… send word to Rithpin, I need as many of his guards as possible surrounding our land… I want every wall including the forest and the secret passage guarded by his soldiers, whether they are good in battle or not I need everyone. I also need the main gate barricaded, we need to keep anything and everything out of our land, now go!" enforced Zanril as he began to announce his plan. "Runil you will go to the Crystállum, you are one of the leaders of this land, protect that crystal with your life!" Zanril continued as he gave orders to his second in command. The room was clearing and soon left only the company and Zanril.

"Can you all fight?" asked Zanril as he looked out of the window still expecting to see Malvo heading towards his land.

"We can, although we don't have as many soldiers as we set out on this quest with, we sadly lost two on our way here, but me Alaya and Elatus have been trained in battle and can handle a sword" replied Pholus,

"What of the earth people?" said Zanril directing a question at the scientists,

"They have no experience of battle, they have weapons, but I am unsure of how well they can use them" replied Pholus,

"We can try, it is my son we are here to save after all, I want to help!" said the Dr with a brave heart,

"I too will help!" Professor Lockley added,

"So will we!" added Michael and Gordon with agreement. The only one not to speak however was Professor Cumbridge, but Dr Stantham had come to expect it from him, so said nothing. The days that had come to pass had truly shown him who were his friends and who were not.

"Very well, we will re-join Rithpin and Norkas… we are of no use hiding in this building. I will die for this land if I need to!" said Zanril before making his way out of the room and back down the stone stairs. The company prepared themselves and readied their weapons including swords, knives and bows and arrows, all of which had been taken from the weapon room of Chiron's home.

"It was a pleasure knowing you gentlemen, and if this is the last day we will spend together, then let it be a good one. We may be scared… and we may be untrained, but we can have peace in the knowledge that we have all become very good friends, and if there had to be something good to come out of this, it would be that you coming here wasn't a complete waste of time after all!" said Alaya expressing the fondness she felt toward her new friends. The scientists smiled in return, touched by her kind words.

"Come, we must join Zanril, he will be waiting for us outside" Pholus added before leading the company out of the room.

The company reached the bottom of the stairs and progressed through the circular hallway, before proceeding to make their way outside. As they stepped outside and back onto the land they saw soldier's running back and forth in blind panic clutching at swords and other items of weaponry fashioned from shining silver steel, untouched and clean. There were also soldiers standing guard at the main gates wearing armour from head to toe and with spears thrust through iron bars prepared for oncoming attacks. Every wall that surrounded the land was accompanied by hundreds of tall, well trained soldiers who stood perfectly still with their sword partly unsheathed with the steel catching the light from above.

"Are you sure you want to be out here scientists?" said Zanril as he gave the scientists one last chance to retreat to a safe haven.

"We are sure!" replied Dr Stantham with a stubborn tone.

Everyone found their positions around the land. The gate had been barricaded and a deathly silence had fallen over every square inch of the once bustling and beautiful realm. The soldiers and the sorcerers and the company of centaurs and scientists waited in angst for the arrival of the enemy. The wait was not a long one however, as Zanril soon noticed in the distance a large shadow of darkness making its way for his land. He could see the outlines of large winged creatures and their black riders,

"They are coming, you were right, I see them in the distance, EVERYONE HOLD YOUR POSITIONS!" shouted Zanril as he announced to all that could hear him that the enemy was only moments away.

***

"I think your friends are having a welcome home party for me, it only seems fitting that we arrive in style, don't you agree human?" said Malvo making a joke at the sorcerers expense.

"Drop dead old man!" snapped Étoile in harsh reply,

"The only one dropping dead today human is you!" replied Malvo tauntingly.

As Malvo drew nearer to the gates of Prévalo, Zanril's soldiers became more aware of the presence of the dark creatures. They were prompted to prepare themselves for attack. All was still hauntingly quiet, like the calm before storm. Then there came the war cry of Zanril echoing through the air.

"HOLD YOUR POSITIONS!" he shouted giving orders to his solders. Norkas, Runil and Rithpin stood near Zanril awaiting the arrival of the black eyed creatures, holding their weapons with sweaty palms and trembling fingers. The black eyed

The Distant Glimmer

soldiers soon became more visible in the gloomy orange sky. Then through the silence the blood curdling voice of Malvo scurried through the air, and signalled the beginning of battle.

"ATTACK!" the war cry was short, yet it was heard rattling through the air calling on his army to make the first move. Still riding upon the backs of the demonic destrier's the black eyed creatures raised their staffs and in an instant the first bouts of electro static energy was forced from their tips. Bolts of lightning and balls of fire were unleashed upon the unsuspecting Prévalo guardsmen.

"They shouldn't have weapons like this… the black eyed beings never had such magic." said Norkas seeming confused.

"It's Malvo, he has introduced them to our own magic, he has supplied them with power and has created an enemy far tougher than we had imagined!" replied Zanril realising that the black eyed beings had evolved. Malvo's soldiers begun destroying the walls that separated the outside world from the Land of the Sorcerers.

Fire balls continued flying overhead and lightning bolts twice as big as the ones they had used before came lashing down upon many of the soldiers killing them instantly. The ground began to shake and the grass and hills were engulfed by flames which spread like a wild fire in a dry forest. Trees burnt to cinders and ash filled the air as sparks flew overhead. The black eyed creatures hadn't even entered the land and already the scene that surrounded the sorcerers looked like that of a battle ground. As the first of the ghost horses touched down inside Zanril's land, they began breathing fire from their nostrils, setting alight more areas of the realm. The black eyed soldiers dismounted the horses and began patrolling the land near Zanril's haven. They continued unleashing bolts of lightning from their staffs, killing and maiming all that stood in their way.

"SOLDIERS… ATTACK!" shouted Zanril as he gave his own battle command. The two armies became locked in battle. The swords the Prévalo guards wielded did not look as if they could match the magical staffs which the black eyed soldiers wielded. However, the expertly trained soldiers of Prévalo began showing skills which were unmatched by Malvo's army. Hope was not yet lost, and the sides were equalled with ability in battle.

Malvo followed his army, and his carriage soon touched down on the ground in the near distance. Dr Stantham made a move to run toward the carriage, but Pholus held him back and warned him of the danger, alerting the Dr. to the substantial amount of guards surrounding the carriage. The scientists were soon greeted with their own problems however as the black eyed soldiers made their way toward them. The scientists had no battle experience, however the anger and adrenaline that coursed through their veins allowed Professor Lockley to strike down one of the black eyed creatures. He stumbled backward with the shock of what he had done. Never before had he taken the life of another, yet the intense situation he was in had hazed his rational mind. He brushed himself off and claimed the magical staff that the creature had once wielded, as his own.

Professor Lockley looked at the staff and tried to determine how to use it.

"Be careful professor, dark magic helped create that!" said Zanril warning Professor Lockley that it may be best not to use it. However, Professor Lockley proceeded to aim the staff towards one of the black eyed creatures, and to his surprise it used the same magic as Rosina's wand. The staff responded to the thoughts in the professor's mind. He used the staff to summon a mini blizzard from out of the air. His mind raged with the thoughts of the pain the creatures had caused to those he cared for, and the blizzard grew stronger, larger and more fierce. He sent the magical storm heading into the path of a group of black eyed soldiers, and in an instant it engulfed them and sent them soaring into the air. Shock and surprise overcame the professor, but his new found magical ability had him testing out new methods that aided him in destroying the foe.

Elsewhere Professor Cumbridge had retreated once again into hiding. It had become apparent that he was cowardly by nature and did not want to help his friends. The battle raged on without him and Dr Stantham, Michael, Gordon and Professor Lockley continued trying their hardest to defeat their new foes and play their own part in the battle. Alaya, Pholus and Elatus were alongside them thrusting and slicing their swords through the air and unleashing arrows upon the enemy. In the distance surrounded by a dozen armoured soldiers Malvo quietly moved his frail body towards the tall stone building, in search of the Crystállum. Étoile was close behind him with his hands and feet chained. He shuffled across the hard ground whilst being manhandled by one of the large armoured creatures.

"There is my son!" shouted Dr Stantham highlighting to the others the position of Malvo

The Distant Glimmer

and Étoile. Zanril turned and saw Malvo making his way into the tall building.

"MALVO!" Zanril shouted before making his way across the dirt covered ground, that was now riddled with dead bodies. Zanril progressed toward Malvo with a sword and staff clutched tightly in his hands, however, as he made his way across the ground he suddenly felt a heavy blow strike the back of his head. The others watched on powerless to help as Zanril fell unconscious and hit the ground. One of the black eyed soldiers moved in to finish off Zanril, but a quick thinking Professor Lockley used the staff which he had stolen and he struck the creature down with a devastating blow. Rithpin and Norkas ran to Zanril's aid and picked him up to drag him to the safety of the old cabin.

"It's up to us now, we need to go after him!" said Alaya, "Dr, give me the Tarnhelm I will try and get close to Malvo!" Alaya continued.

"NO! If anyone is to do this it will be me…it is my son he has up there!" replied the Dr quite harshly.

"We will all go, keep the Tarnhelm with you, Professor Lockley has one of their staffs, we all have swords and knives, if we work together as a team we can take him and those creatures down" said Pholus.

***

Within the boundaries of Zanril's building, Malvo and four armoured black eyed soldiers were leading Étoile up the long winding staircase.

"Keep moving human!" said one of the tall soldiers before pushing its long pale fingers into Étoile's back. Étoile looked pale as the reality and realisation of where he was heading had dawned on him. The hope he once had of being saved had diminished. Malvo walked cautiously up stone steps, panting and growing tired as he progressed. He was drawing nearer to deaths door, and his crooked and aged frame no longer made him look like a powerful and malignant dark wizard. Some Prévalo soldiers suddenly stormed into the building to try and prevent Malvo from reaching the roof, but the black eyed creatures were prepared, and they killed the soldiers with an unnatural ease.

Malvo eventually reached a door at the very top of the building. An unnatural light seeped through the cracks in the doorway and a cold draft howled through the building. One of the soldiers pushed open the doorway, and a blinding flash of light escaped onto the stairway. Runil stood behind the door guarding the Crystállum. He sent spells and curses at the door in the direction hoping to stop them.

"Malvo I know you're there, show yourself, give up whilst you still have the chance!" said Runil trying his best to reason with Malvo. Malvo stepped onto the roof and saw Runil standing there with his wand thrust into the air. Runil clutched his wand so tight that his knuckles had turned white. Malvo's eyebrows were almost concealing his eyes as he frowned at Runil, and his eyes were dark and preternatural.

"Runil, my old friend, how are you? Long-time no see. The last time we were this close was when you were banishing me from my home… from my friends and from my fans, you and the other two old fools. You took everything I had and destroyed it. You left me nothing except a cursed, half-life!" said Malvo with his old weakening eyes fixated on Runil. Runil seemed to feel for the old man, but only for a moment.

"It was your own fault Malvo, you were the one who began using dark magic, you brought this fate upon yourself!" replied Runil as his hands began to shake involuntarily with fear.

"You leave me no choice Malvo, you must be removed from this world!" said Runil before raising his wand and aiming it at Malvo. All Malvo did was smile. Two of the black eyed creatures stepped out from behind the door and met with Malvo on the roof in front of Runil, and before Runil had chance to use his wand to strike Malvo, the two demented creatures unleashed bolts of energy upon Runil. Every cell of his being was destroyed by electro static energy. Runil stood on the spot trembling and foaming at the mouth before finally falling backward. He misplaced his footing and fell from the roof.

***

As the company made their way across the battle ground beneath, they stopped and watched as they saw the body of Runil falling and pulsating with bright blue bolts of energy. They watched as he continued falling until finally his fight for life was over.

THE DISTANT GLIMMER

"No! Runil! Malvo has reached the roof, we must go quickly, your son will be in danger Dr!" said Pholus before prompting the others to follow him. The battle continued around them but they forcefully made their way through it letting nothing stop their progression toward Zanril's building. The world felt to them as if it were playing out in slow motion as they walked across the battle field. Étoile was in danger, and their determination for getting him back was ruthless.

***

"There it is! My power…my work…. my life, all in that crystal!" said Malvo as he stepped forth and peered at the large clear crystal. The crystal gleamed so bright it was unbearable to look at. It was the one magical implement that for so long had been pitting the light against the dark, and had caused too many battles of good versus evil. The crystal rested upon a golden stand centralized on the roof of Zanril's building. The stand that the crystal rested upon had been carved into the shape of dragons claws which caressed the crystal with a delicate touch. The detail was minutiae, and it had been expertly crafted from pure solid gold. The

Crystállum didn't look visually dissimilar to the crystal ball which Aldrien had once used to foresee the future, but it was much bigger, and within it were contained various colours that swirled around with a hypnotic and majestic motion.

"Soldiers! Bring me the human!" snapped Malvo as he turned to give orders to his two black eyed servants. They followed their orders and proceeded to re-open the door on the roof and cease hold of Étoile. Étoile finally had his first glimpse of the magical implement that had caused so much pain and heartache. Two black eyed soldiers stood guard outside the door with their staffs primed for attack.

***

The company led by Pholus made their way back into the lobby of Zanril's building. The sounds of battle could still be heard outside, and the many soldiers of Zanril and the black eyed beings were raging on with no signs of stopping.

"They have made their way to the roof, they haven't seen us yet, but I can see two of those creatures standing guard outside the doorway," said Pholus as he surveyed the area.

"Give me the Tarnhelm Dr!" said Pholus as he reached his hand out,

"I said I would do this!" replied the Dr, feeling reluctant to hand it over,

"I will wear this and kill those guards at the door, it then leaves the entrance open for the rest of you to get onto the roof and stop the old man…please do as I ask!" continued Pholus sounding authoritative.

***

On the roof Malvo, Étoile and two of the black eyed creatures were alone with the battle sounding muffled in the distance.

"Well human, it's time for you to play your part in my plan…. grab him!" Malvo said forcibly. The two black eyed beings moved forth and grabbed one of Étoile's arms. They pushed him forward towards the crystal and held his hands down on the cold, hard surface of the spherical implement. Étoile felt a force rush through his body and his hands felt as if they were being pulled down toward the ground. He couldn't move or pull away no matter how much he fought. Malvo turned to face Étoile and placed his hands on Étoile's head. Once again Étoile tried to fight him off but with a lack of movement is fight proved pointless.

***

    Pholus began quietly making his way up the stairway, step by step. He wore the Tarnhelm which had hidden his physical presence from the guards at the door. He edged his way closer to the two black eyed beings, in one hand he held a sword and in the other he grasped a knife. His heart was racing and he found it hard to swallow. He soon reached the highest level and came face to face with the black eyed creatures, both of whom were still unaware of his presence. Pholus dug deep and found enough courage within his large heart to lunge forth and drive his sword through one of the creatures. It fell to the floor before rolling off the side of the barrier less stairway. Its body greeted the rest of the company in the lobby, and it lay, lifeless and dormant in front of Michael. The second was now on edge and knew someone was nearby. It began lashing out with its staff hoping to strike, whoever or whatever, it was that moved around unseen. Professor Lockley suddenly began running up the steps to the aid of Pholus. Pholus still invisible to the creature knelt down and sliced its knee, Professor Lockley came running up the stairs and used the staff to force the creature against the door before sending it down into the lobby to lay next to its comrade. Pholus removed the Tarnhelm and became visible once again. He wiped sweat from his brow and huffed with a disapproving sigh toward professor Lockley.

***

"What was that? One of you deal with it, the other hold him down, I need to recite the incantation to transfer his life into me" said Malvo as he became anxious.

***

The remainder of the company made their way up the steps to re-join with Pholus and Professor Lockley. Suddenly another of Malvo's soldiers opened the door and saw the company standing on the stairway.

"We have guests master, three centaurs and four more humans" said the creature. Malvo looked worried and expressed a look of panic that Étoile hadn't seen him express before.

"Deal with them!" Malvo shouted with agitation, "and I don't care how!" Malvo added before returning his attention to Étoile. He grasped hold tightly of Étoile's head and began reciting an incantation in the language of the old age sorcerers;

Otanvaltuudetkristalli, joka on,
Täällä nyt edessäni,
Otansielu toisen täällä nyt,
Suo minullevoimaa, Etta sallitte,

As the incantation was read aloud Étoile began to feel weaker and weaker and it was noticeable that Malvo was becoming stronger. His complexion became less pale and his backbone began to straighten. The mist within the Crystállum turned dark red like the colour of crimson blood. The crystals power became stronger as Malvo spoke more and more of the ancient words. Malvo's soldier made its way out onto the stairway and tried to deal with the company single handed. Professor Lockley however, was poised and ready to attack with the staff that he had become all too familiar with. He raised the wooden implement and a black smoke engulfed the creature. Then it was gone. Pholus barged through the doorway and onto the roof. The roof overlooked the entirety of the realm. The battle continued down below with many wounded soldiers still fighting for their lives.

"You couldn't just wait could you, I only needed one human, trust me to get a whole bunch of you!" said Malvo with increasing annoyance in his voice,

"Let my son go!" Dr Stantham demanded.

"Deal with them" said Malvo as he tried to get his final guard to take out the company, but unexpectedly the black eyed creature fled, pushing its way passed Professor Lockley and Pholus before fleeing down the stairs.

Pholus grinned trying to intimidate Malvo, and Étoile stumbled backwards and fell to the ground. The Dr moved across and tried to support him by putting his arms around the back of his head, and Professor Lockley raised the staff and aimed it towards Malvo.

"I don't think so human!" said Malvo before raising his own staff and forcing a spell upon Professor Lockley. The professor dropped the staff and fell to the floor only marginally missing the edge of the roof.

"Get back all of you!" said Malvo still clutching his staff and aiming it at the others.

"I said you wouldn't succeed old man, I warned you, how could you ever think this would have worked out in your favour" said Étoile with what little energy he had left. Étoile looked up at Malvo from the comfort of his father's arms, he looked dirty and bruised and struggled to move.

"Silence human! I said you would die here today and die you shall!" replied Malvo moving his staff and aiming it towards Étoile. Professor Lockley silently moved across the roof and reclaimed the staff. He aimed it at Malvo and sent a spell pulsing toward him. It latched onto the old man and suspended him in the air just beyond the boundaries of the roof. Dr. Stantham stood up and stared into Malvo's eyes,

"And we said we would finish this quest and kill you old man…and kill you we shall!" Professor Lockley then released Malvo from his suspended state high up above the hard ground below. Malvo expelled an involuntary scream before falling beyond the sight of the company. He made fast progression towards the ground. He finally lay defeated and lifeless among the wounded with the battle still raging on around him. Malvo met his demise at the foot of Zanril's home.

On the roof Étoile and Dr Stantham exchanged a smile and a sigh of relief as did the others. Pholus walked to the edge of the roof and shouted down to the black eyed beings below,

"YOUR MASTER IS DEAD, RETREAT NOW OR FACE THE SAME FATE!" the battle immediately came to a halt and the creatures acknowledged the warning. They fled the scene, leaving behind the corpse of Malvo, which now looked unimportant and weak.

19

Friend or Foe?

"It is only the dead that truly see an end to war."

Many of the wounded retreated indoors to rest and find bandages for their fresh wounds. Some of them also sat down where they had once been stood as they didn't even have enough energy to move. Rithpin came from outside the wooden cabin and met with the company who were now making their way once again through the dead bodies. They all looked dirty, scratched, tired and in need of rest and recuperation.

"Thank goodness you are all ok" said Rithpin with a hint of relief.

"Yes, thank you Rithpin, how is Zanril?" asked Pholus as he felt concerned about his wellbeing,

"He is fine, a little bruised… but fine, he is resting in the cabin, I kept him in there out of the way during the battle" replied Rithpin, "please come and see him before you leave" he continued. The company made their way into the cabin and saw Zanril resting with Norkas by his side,

"My friends, you are all well?" Zanril asked trying his best to speak with slurred words,

"We are, we will be returning home now, the Crystállum is safe and we have also saved the life of my friend's son," Pholus replied speaking on behalf of the company,

"It has been a pleasure meeting you all, and thank you for the warning, without it we would have been sitting ducks whilst Malvo attacked us, you have also protected the Crystállum and our world is able to keep its most valuable source of light, I thank you once more my friends" said Zanril as he expressed the gratitude he felt towards the company. The company bid the sorcerers farewell and left them to clear the mess that had been left behind from the battle. The company set off to journey the long way around back to Valosia. The journey ahead was to be another long one, but at least they now walked with peace in their minds. Professor Cumbridge had somehow re-joined the others after having hidden during the entire battle. He was not welcomed back with open arms but was allowed to walk alongside them all the same.

15 hours later:

    Valosia was back in their sites once again, and was exactly as they had left it. The waterfall flowed gently into the stream below, and slowly passed the resting place of the great Chiron. The archway was still a pile of crumbled rock and was in need of repair, but the civilisation of centaurs were the happiest they had been for days. Valosia looked cleaner and most of the rubble and blood stained marble had been cleaned away and all was returning to its original state of beauty.

    "Have they even realised we have gone?" said Alaya with a smile. The company made their way into Valosia and towards Alaya's home, smiling as they went and greeting fellow occupants of the realm, whom Elatus and Alaya had known for many years. The company made their way inside the house and went immediately to the dining room where they had once eaten meals alongside Chiron that had been served up by Bokin the housekeeper.

"Will you all be staying here for the duration?" Alaya asked the scientists,

"I see no reason why not, me and Étoile have already discussed the fact that we have no one else on earth. You are all more of a family to us than we have had in a long time" said Dr Stantham with a nod of agreement from Étoile.

"We too would like to stay if it pleases you, I would rather live a life here, than a secluded and lonesome life back home" said Michael on behalf of both him and his brother Gordon.

"I will also stay, I feel you may need someone with superior intellect and bravery around here" said Professor Lockley jokingly. The mood of the company seemed lighter than it had been for a long time, and everyone had become settled and comfortable in each other's company. That was all except for Professor Cumbridge who didn't seem as happy as the others.

"I am afraid that I do not wish to stay. I know I have made it quite clear on this journey that I have not wanted to be here, I miss home, I miss earth and people!" said Professor Cumbridge,

"Yes you have made it quite clear how it is you feel. However, it is a long journey home, are you certain it is a journey you wish to make alone, in such a large craft!" replied Dr Stantham,

"I am more than certain sir, I am trained for a one man flight. I apologise if my decision displeases any of you, however, I cannot stay, I have too much back home that I wish not to let go of! " replied professor Cumbridge.

The others agreed to respect his wishes and the following day after a long night of much needed rest, they made their way back into the Teumessian forest.

"This is where you landed, the Teumessian Forest, we mustn't stay here long, the foxes are sure to be close by!" said Alaya with some fear in her voice. The space craft stood amidst the trees, and was untouched. Its condition was the same as when it had been left by the scientists, and the shining metal exterior captured and reflected the light of the far away Crystállum. Fallen red leaves also littered the front windows and some trees were leaning against the door. Professor Cumbridge used the remote access key which Dr. Stantham had handed to him and he eventually made his way up the ramp of the craft. Before entering the craft he turned and looked once more at the company who stood together watching him with dejection.

"I am sorry I have not been very co-operative on this journey, but I am afraid I have regret for coming here. I love the planet I come from and there has to be someone to return there to explain to the curious people what has happened to all of you. After a while they are sure to grow suspicious of where their team leader has gone" said Professor Cumbridge with a quick glance at Dr Stantham.

" I understand my friend, it is your choice to return home, and as we have a way of making that possible then return home you shall" replied the Dr.

"Goodbye Michael, Gordon, Professor Lockley and of course Étoile, and goodbye to you my new friends, I am still glad to have met you no matter how much I regretted my prior decisions." said Professor Cumbridge before smiling and finally making his way aboard the craft. Everyone took a few steps backwards before the ion drive of the technically advanced space craft forced itself back into action with a deafening groan. The craft lifted gracefully from the ground with an invisible force, and within seconds, it was gone. It pierced the atmosphere of the planet and made its way through the stars on its course back towards earth. The scientists and the centaurs watched from the surface of the new planet as Professor Cumbridge left them all behind.

"Come, let us go back, I don't know about you but I am hungry, perhaps Bokin can rustle us something up, I hope he doesn't mind cooking for a few extra mouths." said Alaya light-heartedly.

"Could you tell me something Alaya?" said Michael as he walked alongside her,

"Of course, you are part of the family now… ask as many questions as you like my friend" Alaya replied,

"Our home planet is called earth, and this planet is supposed to be its sister is not, however, nobody ever actually said what this planet is called" said Michael curious about the name of the planet he would now call home.

"This planet?, well, it is the planet Orbis!" Alaya replied with a smile reaching across her face. Michael returned the smile and continued to walk with the others on the way back to Valosia.

***

The Distant Glimmer

Zanril, Norkas and Runil travelled a long journey of their own on horseback across the rocky terrain of the planet Orbis. They had the body of Malvo strapped to one of the horses that walked alongside them, as they headed toward the shadowed land. They were returning the corpse to its home as they did not want to be the ones to dispose of it. Malvo was cursed and was one of the black eyed beings. They reached Murdreddia and left Malvo's body outside the wooden gates of the dark realm. His body had been wrapped tightly in a brown sack and left on the dirt beneath the darkness of the black trees; to rot away if no one came collect him. Zanril knocked on the door to gain the attention of the creatures within, before signalling for Norkas and Runil to turn back and journey home to Prévalo. Their journey had been long, and it would be an even longer one by the time they reached home again, but their minds now also felt more at peace having ridden themselves of the cursed old man which had plagued them for so long.

***

THE ORBIS CHRONICLES

8th July 2062, 00:05am

A heavy knock came on the door of the commander's office. It was late into the night, and the mahogany grandfather clock which stood adjacent to a coal fire had only recently struck midnight. It was nearing the time for the commander to return home, but he allowed the person into his office none the less.

"Come in!" instructed the quiet and tired voice of the commander. A trembling hand crept around the door and pushed it open following the granted permission to enter.

"Hello Sir, could I have a word? There is something I need to tell you… you may not understand at first but you need to listen to me,"

"What are talking about?" replied the commander as he sat looking at the man who had entered the office with an incredulous look upon his face.

"A new planet has been discovered by the Krupto initiative…and there is something on it which I think might be of interest to you, it could quite possibly affect the future of our world!"

"I don't understand, how could you know what is on this new planet? And what is powerful?" replied a confused and dumbfounded commander Leatherby.

"It's a long story Sir!"

"Then sit down and explain yourself, you are making very little sense, tell me all you know!" said the commander with anxiousness and with his tiredness forgotten.

"Of course Sir… it will all become clear soon enough!" replied Professor Cumbridge as he found a seat in front of the commander's desk.

THE ORBIS CHRONICLES

The Characters:

The Scientists:

Professor Quinn Lockley

Dr. Bernard Stantham

Professor John Cumbridge

Étoile Stantham

Michael and Gordon Carlson

Akaz and the Red Soldiers:

Akaz: first in command

Brimir: second in command

Gallar

Helgrind

Kolga

Runa

The Orbis Chronicles

CENTAURS:

Chiron: Leader of Valosia

Alaya

Pholus

Elatus

Nessus

Bienor

MYTHICAL CREATURES:

Teumessian Fox

Trodge and Tarcus the mountain trolls

The Three Cyclopes

The Sirens

THE WITCHES:

Rosina

Aldrien

THE SORCERERS:

Rithpin: The Prévalo Gatekeeper

Zanril the leader of the high council

Norkas

Runil

FRIENDLIES:

Bokin: servant of the House of Chiron

John Longwood: guardian of Smugglers Cove

ENEMIES OF THE COMPANY:

Malvo: Powerful sorcerer of dark magic

The Black Eyed Creatures

The Orbis Chronicles

Orbis Realms and Locations:

Teumessian Forest:

Home of the Teumessian Foxes.

Valosia:

Home of the Centaurs.

Murdreddia: The Shadowed Land:

Home of the Black Eyed Creatures.

Eldrador:

Home of the Witches.

Drakontos:

Home of the Dragons.

Gigantria:

Home of the Giants.

Mount Malevolence:

Home of the Mountain Trolls.

Smugglers Cove:

Guarded by John Longwood and home to strange mutant creatures.

Sea of Sirens:

Home of the Sirens.

Prévalo: Land of the sorcerers:

Home of the Sorcerers and the high council.

The Orbis Chronicles

GLOSSARY:

BLACK EYED CREATURES:

Usually, the Black Eyed Creatures has very pale or sickly-looking skin, and very dark hair. They have almost fully black eyes apart from the Sclera of the eye. They are usually men, but not always, and often wear all black or very dark clothes.

CRYSTÁLLUM:

Magical crystal able to take the life of one person and give it to another, also acts as a powerful source of light. (Created solely for this story)

CENTAUR:

A centaur is a mythological creature with the head, arms, and torso of a human and the body and legs of a horse.

Cyclopes:

A Cyclops, in mythology and later Roman mythology, was a member of a primordial race of giants, each with a single eye in the middle of its forehead. The name is widely thought to mean "round-eyed" or "circle-eyed".

Goblin:

They are attributed with various (sometimes conflicting) abilities, temperaments and appearances depending on the story and country of origin. In some cases, goblins have been classified as constantly annoying little creatures somewhat related to the gnome. They also often are said to possess various magical abilities. They are also very greedy and love money.

Sirens:

The sirens were dangerous and beautiful creatures, portrayed as females who lured nearby sailors with their enchanting music and voices to shipwreck on the rocky coast of their island.

Soothsayer:

One who claims to be able to foretell events or predict the future; a seer.

Speculum:

An item that is used to aid a soothsayer in predicting and seeing future events, can be a crystal ball or shiny stone, it can be anything with a reflective surface.

Sorcerer:

A magician or sorcerer is someone who uses or practices magic that derives
from supernatural or occult sources. Magicians are common figures in works of fantasy, such
as fantasy literature, and they draw on a history of such people in mythology, legends and fiction.

Tarnhelm:

THE DISTANT GLIMMER

A Tarnhelm is the name given to a magical helmet that allows its wearer to use it as a cloak of invisibility or change their physical form.

WITCH:

A witch is a man or woman claiming or popularly believed to possess magical powers and practice sorcery.

WAND:

A wand is a thin, straight, hand-held stick or rod made of wood, stone, ivory,
or metals like gold or silver. Generally, in modern language, wands are ceremonial and have associations with magic and are used in order to perform spells and practice witchcraft. They are most likely to be used by a witch or a wizard, and are seen in works of literature relating to magic and fantasy.

The Orbis Chronicles

About the Author

Christopher Mark Stokes was born on 8th January and currently resides in Walsall in the West Midlands. After attaining his GCSE's and also finishing his A-Level studies he decided to try and turn a life-long passion for writing into a career. With the constant support from his family Chris has been able to complete two novels in the fantasy and horror genres. Chris has also used his passion for art in order to create a plethora of illustrated children's books aimed at a variety of age groups, from two year olds to twelve year olds. Chris loves all things in relation to science fiction and horror. Inspirations for his work are authors such as George R.R Martin, J.R.R Tolkien and children's author Roald Dahl. He is also inspired by illustrator Quentin Blake.

Lightning Source UK Ltd.
Milton Keynes UK
UKOW04n0411250615

254080UK00002B/7/P